DREAM OF ME THIS CHRISTMAS EVE

STAR LIGHT ~ STAR BRIGHT SERIES BOOK FOUR

L. A. SARTOR

QUOTE

Star Light, Star Bright
The First Star I See Tonight,
I Wish I May, I Wish I Might,
Have The Wish I Wish Tonight
~ anonymous

DEDICATION

For my brother Jim, with whom I have shared so many Christmas memories. Remember Dad's footprints of ashes on the carpet in California to look like Santa arrived? Remember the snow falls and the bright Christmas morns in Colorado? Our special Christmas tree ornaments? I love you.

And to my readers who asked for Caro's story. This is for you.

CONTROLLED CHAOS RULED THE PAST FEW HOURS. HECK, THE PAST few days.

Caroline Young's most important production was about to begin. Love was definitely in the air. She inhaled the fresh scents of gardenias and eucalyptus and tried to relax by remembering how this all began.

When she'd learned that children's author Annie Hamilton had fallen for Cole Evans, a widower with two young boys, Caro believed their story was the epitome of a happily ever after. Then an extra layer of joy was added as she watched Cole's brother-in-law Mitchell go from being the most negative man on the planet to a smiling best man. But Brice, the brother Caro adored, had stunned them all by thawing the Ice Queen, Jennifer Malone, who just happened to be Annie's best friend.

Caro had organized and monitored everything for the double wedding. From setting up the ginormous white tent two days ago to decorating its cavernous interior. Then making sure luxury Porta-Potties and the standby generator, which were delivered yesterday and would be working under less than ideal weather conditions, wouldn't fail, and if they did, how to troubleshoot.

Yes, this wedding used both her engineering degree and her float-building skills.

She was in her elements.

This morning she was up at five checking her lists and plans, ready for the caterers, the two coat-check attendants, and the valets. Before she dressed in her pale gray-blue silk gown, she turned on each of the table's three candles so the flickering faux flames would give extra ambiance, and if needed, just enough light for the few seconds it'd take the generator to take over if indeed the power went out.

Stop. The moment is near. Just stop.

Caro knew everything that could be under her control was taken care of. And she'd created contingencies for problems. The snow that continued to fall, while gorgeous, added a major headache to the day.

Then again, it was mid-December in Boulder, Colorado, and it snowed here.

Fidgeting with her bridesmaid bouquet, then checking the clock she'd placed discreetly at the entrance to the tent, she saw it was finally 12 p.m. sharp. A second later she heard her cue as RJ, their good friend and pianist for the ceremony, switched from playing his soft piano music and started playing Clarke's Trumpet Voluntary. It was time.

Caro turned and looked behind her. First stood Cole's boys, Josh and Peter, followed by the brides. "Are you ready?" she whispered to Jennifer and Annie.

"Couldn't have done it without you, wild child," Jen teased.

"Seriously?" Caro rolled her eyes. "I thought that name was dead and buried."

Feeling a tug on her dress, Caro looked down.

"What's a wild child?" Josh asked.

Caro widened her eyes and stared hard at Jen, who winked in reply, before answering the boy. "I'll tell you later."

"Okay."

She took a deep breath, knowing this was going to be an incredible day.

Grinning, she directed the boys, looking serious and adorable in their gray suits, to begin. Each had the duty of being a ring bearer for one couple. She followed behind them, starting her step-pause-step cadence down the white, fabric-covered aisle.

Caro's smile widened as she saw her brother standing on the grooms' side, craning his neck to look behind her. He obviously couldn't wait to see his bride, Jennifer Malone.

Beside him stood Cole, impatiently waiting for his bride, Annie Hamilton.

Reaching the altar Caro had decorated with fairy lights, pine boughs, white gardenias and Phalaenopsis orchids, silvery eucalyptus leaves and swaths of silver netting, the boys stood next to the grooms and their uncle Mitchell, acting as dual best man. She moved to the brides' side.

RJ paused for a beat, then played fortissimo, and the two hundred guests rose to honor the two brides, best friends since childhood, as they started down the aisle, side by side.

Caro knew that neither of the women had plans to fall in love and get married. Cupid had other ideas. She'd heard both the couples' stories several times, and it never ceased to amaze her that people could fall in love in such a short time. She'd stopped believing in fairy tales about the age of ten. Yet, here was her brother with Jen, and Cole with Annie.

Just before the brides arrived at the altar, Caro glanced at her parents in the front row. Her mom fumbled with the white hanky Dad handed her, then wiped away tears of joy. They too had fallen in love quickly in the small Kansas town where Caro and Brice had grown up.

Caro returned her attention to the couples in front of her and took the two bouquets, stepping back as the grooms joined their brides.

RJ rose from the piano and stood before them. He'd been ordained especially for this day.

This wedding, a week shy of Christmas, had been in the planning stages for about six months. Caro would have dropped any clients for Forever Young, her business, that wouldn't allow her the luxury of a week off from their projects to attend this celebration. Last year she'd had her first float in the prestigious Rose Bowl parade in Pasadena and even won an award for it. She had another one for the parade a year away, but from a couple of days ago to December twenty-seventh, she had a clean slate and promised to spend Christmas in Boulder.

Her dance card was full with a crazy, demanding job, but one she loved.

Her attention focused back on the wedding as Brice took a ring from Josh, Cole's youngest son.

"You are my life, my love. Forever is not long enough to show you the depth of my admiration and love for you," her brother vowed to his beloved.

He slipped the ring on Jennifer's finger and swept her into a dip-style kiss.

The guests applauded and hooted, then Jennifer and Brice, hand in hand, stepped aside, making room for Annie, Cole, and the boys to stand in front of RJ.

Cole clasped Annie's hands. "Annie, Josh and Peter adore you. I love you and believe I'm the luckiest man in the world to have you by our sides, in our lives, believing in our dreams as we move through life together," Cole vowed.

Peter handed Cole a ring, and he slipped it on Annie's finger, then kissed her soundly. She bent to embrace the boys and give them each a kiss.

Tears unexpectedly flooded Caro's eyes at the bounty of love that emanated from this tiny spot in the universe.

The lights in the chandeliers flickered and, much to her relief, stayed lit. RJ played a rousing tune as the couples, followed by the boys, then Caro, with her hand tucked in Mitchell's arm, walked up the aisle.

Just before she ducked into the house, Caro heard RJ announce to the guests that while the couple signed documents and the chairs were being moved to the tables, the wine bar and coffee bar were open if people would like to enjoy.

She followed the wedding party into Jennifer's dining room. As she was adding her witness signature to each of the documents, the lights flickered once again, then stayed off.

MAXIMILLIAN HENDERSON III ADMIRED HOW THE CAVERNOUS TENT filled with two hundred-plus guests felt intimate, yet exotic.

His sense of aesthetics approved of the eucalyptus garlands snaking down the center of the oak tables. White blooms of some sort and ribbons of silver netting intertwined with the best faux candles he'd ever seen casting their flickering light. China, silverware, and soft white linen napkins sat on oak tables.

The effect was both elegant and eclectic.

As was the creator of all this, bridesmaid Caroline Young in her filmy gown and tumbled fiery hair.

Max was Jen's next-door neighbor, and when Brice had come into the picture, they'd become friends. Often, over dinner, drinks, or a movie trivia night, Brice talked about his sister and had proudly shown Max many pictures of her.

He'd been fascinated by the way she so easily, and with

insouciance, wore combinations of patterns, textures, and colors. None of the woman he knew could carry off the bohemian look that flattered this fiery sprite.

In fact, he recognized a bit of envy in his admiration of her. He wore suits to work and well-thought-out casual clothes, and pretty much everything he wore matched. Her "look" felt much more carefree than his attorney persona would allow. And damn if he didn't admire her freedom to dress as she chose. Maybe if he could spend a bit of time with her, it'd rub off on him.

Max, old man, you've carefully cultivated this attorney persona. Don't forget that.

Right. Yet her magic lingered as he looked down at his dark suit, then thought of her in her flowing maid-of-honor gown.

Damn, now you're being fanciful.

Suddenly, the chandeliers in the tent flickered, then went dark, the only light now twinkling from the candles on the tables and wan winter light coming from the tent's clear plastic windows. Murmurs around him were more curious than anxious.

Moments later, through the windows Max saw Caro moving like a wisp of gray smoke along the outside of the tent. She'd donned a gray sweater over her gown and covered her hair with a muffler of some sort.

Then she disappeared from sight as the falling snow enveloped her. What the heck was she doing?

Instantly he was on his feet and headed through the nearly invisible door at the back of the tent. Spur of the moment wasn't his style. Nothing about Caro was his style, yet he felt suddenly and completely protective of her. It was bitterly cold, still snowing, and she was out there alone.

And on top of his worry, there was something about her that spiraled a tendril of desire through him. Just a hint, nothing he could pin down, but enough to add urgency to his quest.

Snow immediately filled his shoes and came midway up his calves as he forged a path through the virgin snow, heading in the direction he last saw Caro take. Finally, he was on the plowed driveway and could now make time as he passed the trailer of fancy Porta-Potties. A few feet beyond that and he was back in deeper snow.

Following the trail of footsteps, he finally found Caro bending over a mammoth generator, which thankfully was running. Yet she remained beside it.

"Need some help?"

She looked up, then dusted her hands off and tucked them beneath her sweater.

"Nope, think I found the issue. The Porta-Potti wagon must have rolled over the electrical cord enough to pull it from its emergency socket. The power should be on by now."

She made a move to retrace her steps to check on the lights in the tent when he saw her shiver. He at least had on a wool suit coat. And while her sweater looked warm, the gray dress beneath it didn't. "I'll go look, you head to Jennifer's lab and get warm before we head back."

"I've got on boots—you don't. But I would like to double-check a couple things on my planning board, so thank you."

He looked down, and damn if she didn't have on heavy boots under her bridesmaid gown. "I'll meet you at the lab in a minute."

"I don't need you to—"

Max didn't wait to hear her answer as he retraced his steps far enough to see the lights in the tent. He could go on and enjoy the party, as he was sure Caro had been going to say, yet he paused.

What on earth caused that? Was it the emotion of the double wedding, the closeness of Christmas? Whatever the reason, desire to know Caro a whole lot better struck him hard.

He waited in the falling snow and bitter cold to see if his desire to be near her still hammered at him, and realized it hammered harder.

Okay then. Back to Jen's pool house, which she'd turned into a mini version of her forensics office she called the lab.

He entered quietly and softly shut the door behind him. Caroline hadn't heard him, thus offering him time to study her. She'd pulled off the muffler and wore her hair in a messy sort of style, while an embroidered headband studded with gemstones of some sort held the fiery mass off her face. The bluish gray of her gown fit her style perfectly.

While she appeared delicate, he knew otherwise from the times Brice had talked about her welding part of a float if she was short a person or climbing up on the skeleton to add the wire mesh that would hold the flowers. Or driving hell-bent through a corn field in Kansas as a teenager.

Brice called her a wild child.

Max's glance flicked over to the wall to see what she appeared to be engrossed in. Flow charts, lists, and schematics covered the entire wall over the desk. "This looks like a battle plan."

Caro turned, and her smile practically knocked him backward. It was completely genuine all the way to the sparkle in her gray eyes. She was obviously in her element. He understood, for he felt that way when he won a case or created a complex trust or complicated real estate lease.

Her energy drew him closer, and he had to stop from touching her, though his fingers itched to trace the column of her throat to her jaw and then down again, to her—

"Well, since I couldn't talk either couple out of a winter wedding, I had to plan for every contingency." She waved her hands toward the wall of plans and charts.

Max stepped even closer to take a better look.

He studied the plans tacked up and suddenly realized this woman could be exactly what he needed.

Now all he had to do was think of a way to convince her.

"Ready to go back?" he asked, formulating and discarding ideas even as he spoke.

"Yep, but your shoes didn't get dry."

"It's okay, I'll survive."

Caro laughed. A throaty, full-bodied sound he felt all the way to his cold toes.

"Some wine, champagne, and a great meal combined with all this love will warm you up." Caro rose and wrapped her muffler back around her neck and over her head.

"Are you a romantic?"

"Only for other people."

What an odd thing for her to say.

2

HOURS LATER, CARO SLIPPED OFF HER FOUR-INCH HEELS AND PUT her stockinged feet up on the coffee table in Jennifer's living room. Activity bustled around both the house and the tent as the caterers and rental folks were cleaning up and taking down. Right now, they could bustle without her.

After all her job was mostly done. The major players and guests had left.

Annie, with Cole and the boys, had bundled into Mitch's Lexus and headed to DIA for a trip to Hawaii.

Mitch was off to Grand Junction to meet the winner of his blog makeover contest.

Jennifer and Brice had headed somewhere for a honeymoon night, and then back to work tomorrow on a big joint cybersecurity project.

And Mom and Dad had headed back to the Boulderado for a quick nap and then a walk down the Pearl Street Mall and dinner later.

She was supposed to join them for dinner, but right now Caro wanted nothing more than to do nothing. She poured another splash of champagne into her crystal flute from the bottle she'd snagged in the kitchen.

Just as she was about to take a sip, her phone vibrated beside her on the couch. She looked at the screen and a shiver of worry danced up her arms. Jennifer's number.

She grabbed the phone and poked the on button before the call could go to voice mail. "Jen? Everything okay?"

"What? Oh, sure, we're fine. I forgot to tell you that Max is popping over around four to ask you a question."

"Here?"

"Yeah, knowing you, I told him you weren't leaving until the last crumb was cleaned up."

Caro chuckled softly. "True. Any idea what he wants?"

"None, he was very mysterious."

"As are you and Brice. Where are you?"

"Not telling, but nice try. See you tomorrow sometime, or later if you and your folks head up to the mountains tomorrow."

"Um, not in this snow. Mom and Dad have no idea how to drive up steep hills—or down them, which is worse—in this kind of weather."

Caro heard Jen's deep laugh, and then the cell phone connection was broken. She sipped her champagne and wondered what on earth Maximillian Henderson III could possibly want to ask her.

To go out on a dinner date? The thought of the two of them alone quickened her pulse. There was something about him that intrigued her. He was careful with his words, and she figured that was the attorney in him, yet his navy eyes danced when he let his guard down a bit.

She wondered what they'd look like when he was arguing a case or laughing at a joke. Or when he ... Caro blinked and came back to reality. Maximillian Henderson III lived here in Boulder, and she lived and worked in California. Nothing was going to happen between them.

The commotion from the cleanup had died down to the rumble of the huge mobile refrigerators that were being wheeled out. She shivered as a cold draft flowed through the many layers of her chiffon bridesmaid dress, sending goosebumps up her legs. Not feeling the least inclined to get up and change into real clothes, she found the fireplace remote and turned it on, then grabbed the throw so invitingly thrown over the arm of the couch to pull over her chilly legs. The minute her fingers sank into the softness of the vicuña wool, she buried her face in the throw and let loose a loud sigh. How she'd love to knit with something this luxurious.

"Ahem."

Caro looked up, her face still buried in the throw, to find Max standing next to the couch staring down at her with a wicked gleam in his eyes and the smallest of smiles curving his lips.

"Er, caught me in the act." She thrust the throw toward him. "Really, though, feel this."

FEEL THIS? SERIOUSLY, SHE WANTED HIM TO DO WHAT? AFTER that sigh, he wasn't sure he should. "Why are you so excited about an afghan?"

"Not just any old afghan, this one is vicuña. Seriously, feel it."

If he hadn't reached out to take it from her, the throw would have fallen to the floor, and Max had an idea that would have been akin to sacrilege in Caro's eyes.

Despite himself, he held it up to his cheek. Soft, supple ...

Whoa, his thoughts were spinning in wild directions, all because of the woman sitting in front of him. "Nice."

"Nice? Do you know what vicuña is?"

"Nope, can't say that I do."

"It's the wild relative of the llama. Pretty rare these days. The Incas believed the critters were reincarnations of lovely young maidens, so only Incan royalty were allowed to wear the fleece. Their wool is incredibly expensive. Nevertheless, I'd love to find some."

Max handed her back the throw, only to see her again bury her face into its softness. And damn if his body didn't heat up a few degrees thinking about her nuzzling his neck with the same passion. Sucking in a lungful of the chilly air wafting through the front door cleared his mind. Just. "First, how do you know all this? And second, what would you do with the wool if you were to find and then afford it?"

"First, I love random facts. My teachers hated that, especially when I spouted off in class, answering a question with a fact or even another question."

"And yet you were valedictorian of your high school class. Phi Beta Kappa, and *magna cum laude* at university."

"How'd you know?"

"Brice. He talks about you all the time."

"Oh, did he tell you that I knit?" She gestured Vanna White style to the sweater still topping her maid-of-honor gown.

Max felt his brows rise in surprise, and there was nothing he could do to stop his obvious reaction to her last reveal. Knitting seemed like such an old-fashioned art for a free spirit like Caro. He prided himself on reading people—it was one of the traits that made him a successful attorney. Yet Caro, in the past few hours, delivered him one surprise after another. His interest level in her ratcheted up and went beyond his physical attraction.

If she agreed to his plan, this could be an interesting week ahead, matching wits and wherever anything else led. "You read structural and interior design plans, right?"

"I create design plans for structural engineering. So yes."

"My designer has the flu and can't finish the work on my new office building. I could use your expertise to help complete the final phase so it's open by the new year."

"I'm not really an interior designer."

"It's a bit more than that."

"How much more?"

She pulled the afghan up on her lap a little higher and he realized the draft continued.

"Hold on a sec, I'm going to see if the door was left open. It's letting in minus-degree cold."

Everyone had left the house. He closed the slightly ajar door, feeling instantly warmer, then returned to Caro and perched on the sofa's arm.

"Okay, so you're not an interior designer. And you asked how much more."

She nodded, then poured a bit more champagne into her glass and sipped.

"The building is old and I'm having a lot of work done to the interior. And some new windows added. And—"

He stopped when she held up her hand. *Uh oh.*

"I'm not an interior designer, but I do love playing with space and color, fabrics and textures, I do it all the time with my floats. That's what makes them stand out in a crowded field.

"I was going to say, if it's just a matter of placing furniture according to your designer's layout, you won't really need any help. But if it's more structural, electrical and reading plans, it would be interesting to see what you're doing, so I agree." She put the champagne glass on the table.

"To help?"

"Sure. I promised Brice and Jen that I'd stay in Boulder with our folks and celebrate Christmas. It'll be the first full family Christmas in a while. But I can't just sit around and knit all day until I head home. So this will be fun."

"Fun? That's not a word I'd use when it comes to putting all this together."

"I'm sure your designer has a project bible, and I can use it to check all the work schedules and deliveries. And it should list everyone from the painters to the tech guys."

"Tech guys?"

"Surely you're going to or already have had your office wired with the latest and greatest tech."

"Actually, I don't know."

"Did you talk about what you needed with your designer? Like wireless, high-speed Internet, cloud storage, or your own servers?"

"I didn't, but Margo might have."

"Margo?"

"My junior partner, daughter of Howard Stout. The firm is Henderson, Stout and Henderson. Howard passed away a couple of years ago."

"And the first Henderson is your father?"

"Was. He died shortly after I joined the firm." Max stood and looked out the huge windows in Jennifer's living room as the white blanket of snow faded and became instead the narrow white, sterile cubicle, curtained off from the rest of the emergency room at the old Community Hospital. The images flashed into his mind with the same intensity they had ten years ago.

Max reached down and grabbed the champagne glass Caro had set on the coffee table and took a long draw. It didn't matter that it was alcohol in the glass, it mattered only that it was wet and lessened the tightness that suddenly filled his throat.

"Your father must have been young."

"Too young. On a day similar to this, snowing hard, Dad decided to close the firm early and come home as no clients were scheduled. He'd called Mom and told her tonight was perfect for pasta and wine. He never made it. A man who had a five-martini lunch barreled through a busy intersection, T-boning Dad."

"Oh my God, Max, I'm so sorry. For him, for you, your mother, your family."

Caro stood and snaked an arm around him, hugging him tight. He turned his head down to look at her and saw tears shimmering in her gray eyes. One slipped out and trickled down her cheek. Max reached down and gently wiped it away with his thumb.

She reached out and cupped his cheek, then slowly stroked his beard. Hers was a tender touch filled with sympathy and compassion.

Max rested his forehead against hers for a moment, savoring the connection between them. How this could happen so quickly was beyond him, but right now he didn't want to question it.

Unsure how long they stood together, he finally straightened and ran a finger down her cheek, trailing the dried tear track. "Thank you."

Sitting back on the sofa's arm, he sipped from the glass again and handed it back to Caro.

"Why don't you use Margo to help finish up the project?" she asked as she put the glass on the table.

"Are you retracting your yes?"

"No, just trying to understand the setup and the players."

Caro surprised him again. One smart cookie.

"She's in the midst of a trial. The plan was to basically close over the New Year weekend, move the furniture from the old office and open right after the New Year. Margo is my techie attorney and was in on the planning stages of the design and the move."

"Wow, so you are in a bind. I repeat, I'll help as much as you need me, but it really may be a simple put-this-here, that-there type of thing. And your designer may be on her feet soon."

"I have a nasty feeling she's going to retire after this."

"Oh, are you that hard of a boss?"

"Nope, she had hinted it was her last job. So, do you want to come over to the new building and get started?"

"Like now?" Her eyes widened in horror.

"Okay, how about tomorrow, which is Sunday. Nothing is starting until Monday."

"Good. Honestly, I'm too keyed up to concentrate and I'm supposed to meet my parents for dinner, but maybe I'll just have a glass of wine and watch them eat."

"I'll pick you up tomorrow morning, say around nine?"

"Earlier is fine, I'm used to getting up and hitting the day."

"Nine is good. Where are you guys staying?"

"The Boulderado."

"Perfect. We can walk to the new building." He couldn't help it, looking at her high-heel-shod feet. "Those boots you wore earlier, they're yours, I hope."

Her laughter rang out and he smiled in spite of himself.

"Of course they are. I was warned by Brice to come fully equipped for snow. Which, if you know anything about Brice's story, was that he didn't take his own advice and wore loafers to come to Boulder and work with Jen on Vader, that cyber defense project that brought them together. You'd think, as he attended the Air Force Academy in Colorado Springs, he'd have known better. Colorado, winter, and snow are synonymous."

Max laughed at the slight scold in her voice as she talked about Brice. In fact, he and Brice were becoming good friends. A good thing as he was Jen's neighbor and he enjoyed the little time they did get together to chat or enjoy a drink on his or her patio. Then Brice came into the picture and it was a trio that shared those drinks and sometimes a barbeque along with movie tidbits and music trivia.

Caro got up to carry her glass into the kitchen and wash it. Max followed her with the champagne bottle, corked it, and put it in the fridge. "How are you getting back to the hotel?"

"Thought I'd call a cab or a ride share."

"Why don't I take you?"

3

Caro turned over in bed, groaned, and then realized she was awake. Picking up her phone resting on the Victorian-styled nightstand, she read 7:30 a.m. on the face. Way too early to get up, as Max wasn't coming until nine, but sleep had fled.

She'd slept quite soundly in the comfortable hotel bed, which was rare for her. A comfortable bed leading to a good night's sleep was the number one reason she hauled her Airstream trailer to job sites outside her home town of Pasadena. Not only could she sleep in her own bed, she could make the food she loved and have all her equipment around her, creating the environment she needed to do her best work. She couldn't imagine not being able to work that way.

Which was one reason she wasn't looking for a relationship. A casual night out was okay, but anything that could cause her to change her lifestyle or put restrictions in place wasn't going to happen, period.

Max and his problem would be a nice distraction while she stayed her promised time in Boulder.

Deciding she had time for a leisurely bath, she slid out of the bed. Pulling aside the window's blackout curtains, she looked at the scene below her in awe as the beauty of the sunny morning reflected off the huge snow drifts that had settled on the sidewalks and rooftops. It was a truly magnificent, postcard-quality scene.

She couldn't wait to get out there and walk around. But first the bath.

Finding the lovely basket of bath goodies that Jen had given her, she dropped a bath bomb into the steaming water filling the antique, pristine clawfoot tub. Pinning up her hair, Caro slipped into the hot foamy bubbles and realized she was eager to see Max again.

It wasn't as if Maximillian Henderson III was her kind of guy. No, just the opposite. He seemed a bit stuffy, a little too rigid, even if he was absolutely drop-dead gorgeous with that beard and mustache. And his eyes? An impossible shade of deep blue. It was the challenge that drew her. It tickled her to make him laugh and see that very rare twinkle light up his eyes.

And she couldn't wait to see just what he had in mind for his office. She imagined it would be filled with stuffy furniture, bookcases with leather-bound tomes of law, but then again, perhaps she would be pleasantly surprised, and it would be amazing.

She added a bit more hot water to the tub, and as she soaked, she created and discarded ideas for the perfect law office set in Boulder, a trendy, techno-friendly town that still had lovely buildings from the late 1800s.

Caro thought she heard a knock on the door and realized she had no idea what time it was. Then a series of loud staccato raps. Only then did she realize the water was now tepid and the bubbles had dissipated.

It couldn't be nine yet, could it?

Rising from the claw-footed tub took more of an effort than

she realized. It wasn't like stepping out of a shower. Slipping on the thick terry hotel robe, she flew to the door.

"Yes?"

"It's Max."

Opening the door a crack, she peered out, seeing Max dressed in a parka and heavy laced boots with a fleece collar around the edge. Totally ready for their trek to his office.

"Hi. You're early," she punted, not having time to check her phone to see what the time really was.

"No, actually I'm a bit late."

"Have you had breakfast yet?" she asked, hoping he'd say no, which would give her more time to get ready while he ordered breakfast for them in the restaurant downstairs.

"Yes. But I'm guessing you haven't. How much time do you need?"

She grinned at his astuteness and opened the door a bit wider. "I promise, not long."

"How long is not long?"

She caught his swift glance from her wet bare feet up her voluminous white robe to her hair pinned up. Skepticism was written in his brows drawn together, his lips pursed and his eyes —they twinkled. Thank goodness.

"I promise ten minutes tops. Can you order me a double espresso, a muffin, and a bottle of water from the restaurant downstairs? I can eat as we walk. Didn't you say we were walking to your office?"

"Yes and yes."

Max's lip curved up in a smile, and she swore she warmed up ten degrees.

"I'll meet you in the lobby with a to-go bag in hand."

He turned away, then back. "What kind of muffin?"

"I don't care, I love them all. Surprise me."

"I think that might be hard to do."

"Give it a shot." She flashed him her most brilliant smile and closed the door before he had a chance for a comeback. Leaning against it, she realized the smile was still on her face. Okay, then, her time in Boulder was looking up.

MAX TUCKED THE BOTTLE OF WATER INTO HIS POCKET, GRABBED the paper cup of requested espresso with one hand and snagged the bag of muffins with the other, then headed from the restaurant to the lobby.

Caro was as good as her word. She was heading down the grand wooden staircase at the same time.

She glanced at her watch and threw him a smile. "Darn, eleven minutes. I was waiting for an elevator, which seemed as slow as molasses, or I would have made it."

Reaching out for the cup, she took a quick sip just as "careful it's super hot" escaped his lips.

"It's perfect, thank you. But a slight change in plans. Is it all right if I eat the muffin at your office while we look at the plans?"

"Of course." He scanned her from head to toe. A knitted green sweater peeked from beneath her rust-colored down puffy vest. A knitted scarf, this one a darker rust with gold shot through it, wrapped around her neck. Black jeans and pretty serious black boots that came halfway up her calves completed her look.

"Do I meet with your approval?"

Oh yes, those jeans were painted on. "Got a hat?" he asked with a sudden hoarseness that surprised him.

Caro pulled a knitted cap out of her vest's pocket and waved it in his face.

He grinned and loved that she smiled back. Man, she was so different from the women he was usually attracted to. She constantly kept him on his toes. Caro wasn't beige. That's the term he used to describe women who wore impeccably matching outfits, usually in monochrome tones. Nope, everything about Caro was bright and vibrant.

"I thought we'd stop by the new office first and see the plans, then I'll drive us over to the old office and you can see the furniture and equipment.

"Where is the old office?"

"Up on the Hill, University Hill. Dad bought it long ago and it worked great until about eight years ago when parking became a huge issue for our clients. I hated to sell it, but Mom agreed. The new owners are going to turn the lower level into retail shops and turn the upper two floors into apartments."

"For students? Those should do well."

"No, actually for fifty-five-plusers and faculty. They want to expand another floor but are running into road blocks."

"I like that idea. Students from campus, faculty, and wise elders in one neighborhood. Nice mix. Neighbors are one thing I miss, living where I do."

"Where do you live that doesn't have neighbors? Or is it a rough neighborhood?" Damn if his mouth wasn't paying attention to his usual cautious lawyerly nature. And why would he think she'd live in an area that wasn't just like her? Bright and colorful.

Caro's sudden peal of laughter charmed him yet again. "Not a rough neighborhood. You're right, I don't have neighbors. I live in my thirty-foot Airstream and park it behind my combination warehouse-office building."

"Seriously?" He couldn't believe it as he'd just pictured her in a Pasadena bungalow with an abundance of flowers.

"Yeah. It works perfectly for me. Do I detect a note of disapproval with my lifestyle?"

"Heck no—amazement, curiosity, but nothing negative."

"Good, I'd hate to quit your project before I even began."

Her smile lessened the impact of her words, but he received a message loud and clear. DO. NOT. DISS. Or else, no Caro.

"Ready to head out? It's about four degrees below zero, but it's only a block over and a few blocks east on the corner of Mapleton and 17th, so we won't freeze."

"Lead the way."

Opening the door for her with one hand and holding the bag of muffins with the other, he followed her out to 13th Street and headed north. Caro was so aware of her surroundings—it was fun to watch her take in the snow, the Victorian buildings, the Christmas decorations from gaudy to simple.

She tucked her hand into his elbow, and the day felt almost like a vacation day. Free, fun and something new, with more to look forward to.

They reached his new office, and Max looked at it with a different eye, more critical, as if seeing it through Caro's first impression.

"Wow! The outside is to die for. When you said new, I expected a new build. But I love all that old brick. And is the parking lot yours?"

"Yeah, it cost nearly as much as the building, but it'll be worth it."

For some peculiar reason, Max felt he needed to open the door for Caro and quickly extended his hand to beat her to it. "After you."

"Such a gentleman."

"Don't let that get out. I'm a shark in this business. Can't have that image ruined."

"I promise I won't tell a soul."

He stood aside as Caro stepped into the foyer of his—no —*their* new building. Mom had as much at stake as he did.

Stepping around a pile of aluminum struts and a huge stack

of drywall, she put her cup on the temporary table in the middle of the room and turned to face Max. Uh oh, fire blazed in those gray eyes.

"Are you seriously going to cover all this brick with ordinary drywall?"

Hands on her hips, she totally presented the picture of indignant.

"Well, answer her."

Max turned to see his mom standing in the building's doorway, her lips curved into a smile and a quizzical expression in her eyes. One that always meant her opinions were at odds with his.

Just great. Back to the argument he thought he'd won two weeks ago.

"Yes, it's been decided."

"No, it's wrong." Caro twirled around quickly, taking in the entire entry. "That is a huge mistake."

4

"NOT YOU, TOO."

Max looked completely exasperated. Well too darn bad. It would be a mistake to cover these walls.

"Too? As in me and your mom?" Caro guessed and hoped she was correct. The similarities between the woman standing in the doorway and Max were great.

From their dark hair to their stunning navy eyes. Her nose was straighter than his, but their lips were the same. Full. And they were both tall. His mom elegantly so, whereas Max was more solidly built. His abdomen was flat, so unless he was naturally fit, she guessed he worked out.

Caro moved to the door, hand extended. "Hi, I'm Caroline Young. Max asked me to lend a hand with the last stages of getting the office ready as apparently his designer is ill."

"Wow, and you agreed? Geraldine Henderson, and by the way, please call me Geri."

Caro grasped Geri's hand, pleased it was a firm grip. No limp finger-touching that often passed for a handshake, not for this charming woman. Geri exuded style, from her silver parka to her black leggings. And those boots. Knee high with lug soles. Totally perfect.

"So, Debra is still out sick?"

"Hi, Mom, and yes she is. Apparently it's the flu."

"She worked while she was sick, telling you it was a simple cold. And now it's really the flu? And this was her last job. You drive people too hard, you know. One of your few faults." She looked at Caro and back at her son.

Caro kept her expression bland until the grin couldn't remain hidden.

"Mom, Caro's a volunteer. I won't work her into the ground. She's Brice's little sis. And you'll love this. She's an award-winning float designer and engineer. Remember last New Year's Day, when the float you loved won the Princess Award? That was Caro's float."

How did he know all that? Oh, yeah, Brice. "Guess my brother told you?"

"Yup, more than once. He was extremely proud of your first big parade, the Granddaddy, he called it."

"Seriously?" Geri said, her eyes huge. "You and I have to talk. That float was amazing. I was so irritated when the TV cameras moved on to the next one. I want to hear all about it."

Caro grinned again at Max's mom. She'd be fun to spend some time with. "I'd love to chat about what I do, but I warn you, I love my job and you might regret asking."

"I doubt it, but carry on, I want to hear why you think it's a mistake to cover the walls with drywall."

"You mean desecrate them? Max, do you mind if I look upstairs?"

"Sure, have at it."

She climbed the old wooden staircase, hearing it creak on each step. "Are you saving this?"

"Nope. New one is going in after the drywall Wednesday."

Hmmmm, we'll see about that drywall. "What material are you making the new staircase out of?"

"Black iron structure and railings with dark wood steps. Open."

"Modern?"

"Yes. As the walls will be."

"Hmmmm."

Max followed her upstairs with Geri trailing behind.

"What are the offices upstairs?"

"Conference room, library, file room, and now the associates' offices. Debra and I decided on that a week or so ago."

"You expect clients to come up here?"

"No."

"What about future employees that might be unable to climb the stairs? You need to think ADA-compliant stuff."

"Are you talking installing an elevator?"

"Yup. We need to look into that, or maybe you have a variance?"

He looked startled. "Not that I know of, but I'll check with Margo on Monday."

His tech attorney. Well, Caro hoped it was all taken care of.

Reaching the top floor, the full-length windows enchanted her. But they looked single pane and not at all energy efficient.

"Are you changing out the windows?"

"Yep, smaller, more efficient."

"Too bad."

"What now?"

Caro heard the deep rumble of exasperation in Max's voice, but she couldn't stop at this point.

"Efficient is great, smaller will make it darker. And even though you're saving with smaller windows, I bet you're paying more for the contractors to match the exterior brick. And it takes longer. When are they going in?"

"That's why I want you. I don't know the exact timetables. Or much of anything about this."

He sounded harried. Well, if his designer did have a project bible, then Caro would know everything once she'd read it.

Turning to go downstairs, she realized there was a load of drywall up here as well.

"Max, seriously, why are you dry-walling all this gorgeous old brick? It's a sin."

"CARO, THE BRICK LOOKS OLD. I'M TRYING TO LOOK LAWYERLY. We're keeping our leather furniture because people expect lawyers to have it. But I want the rest to look modern. We charge a lot an hour, and I want people to think they're getting the most up-to-date law firm."

Max watched her expression, specifically her lips move from a bland smile to a frown in lightning speed. Obviously bringing her in was a big mistake. One he could rectify right now.

"I think we're on the wrong page here. I just needed some help making sure everything was going smoothly. That the wiring was right, the furniture was placed in position, and we could open on schedule." Yet he couldn't find the right way to tell her she was no longer needed.

His mom had leaned against the window frame and was looking out the window, which he knew gave her a great view of the surrounding snow-clad trees and in the west, the monolithic sandstone Flatirons. He also knew she was biting her tongue. Damn.

Caro tilted her head and surprised him with a smile. "That was the most polite kiss-off I've ever received. But will you at least just give me a few minutes to show you another vision? Is there a warmer room we can use downstairs?"

Max saw her glance his mom's way and realized what Caro was saying. It was cold up here and Mom *was* involved with what was going on, even if she'd basically given him carte blanche.

"Sure, I'd like to hear what you think, but we're on deadline, so ..."

He led the way downstairs and noticed that Caro went right to the temporary table where she'd set her coffee, and without hesitation pulled the stack of blueprints closer and started flipping through them. She stopped on one with the details on the staircase that would replace the old wooden one they'd just descended.

"This new staircase is stunning. Modern, practical, and a great center piece when clients enter the office."

She sat in one of the metal folding chairs, Max in the other, leaving the upholstered club chair for Mom.

"I get what you're trying to do here, but it's a mistake not to go all the way. You started with the staircase, why not continue the theme."

Max bit his tongue and simply motioned with his hand for her to continue.

"What I've noticed about Boulder in the times I've been here is that its backbone is the many charming old buildings all over the city. Yet Boulder also gives off a modern vibe for the up and coming entrepreneurs and high-tech folks that are settling here. Your client base is what? Older? Mixed?"

"Mixed, that's what we're aiming for. In fact, we're looking for an intellectual rights attorney to add to our team."

He'd apparently scored a point with his last comment because Caro's eyes lit up.

"Then show them that you're not stodgy and old school. Let the brick remain just as it is and be the bones of the space. Use enough high-end modern furniture to showcase your up-to-date side. You've already started with the staircase."

Max paced the space between the door and the large table where Caro stood, arms crossed. It sounded interesting but changes of that magnitude this late? "I can't get the office open if we make these changes."

"Of course you can. There will be some additional cost, and I can work up the figures, but you'll save on the drywall. The only biggie is making sure all the wiring and cabling is hidden in channels and up to code. A few closets or armoires can hide all the routers and other electronic needs.

"Imagine walking in the front door and seeing your receptionist behind a fabulous glass desk welcoming your clients. Add some modern leather chairs, sofas, a coffee station with a glass fridge and you've immediately presented a firm that is forward thinking."

Max tamped down his frustration that Caro wasn't getting his concept. "I want people to walk in and think this law firm is grounded and successful, not simply forward thinking. I believe people have expectations about what presents success to them. They come to us to win that case, or be covered by the best contract, or create a trust that will be usable in the future. Clean, bright walls mixed with our furn—"

"Wait, don't tell me. Let me tell you what I think you're bringing in."

A slight laugh covered by a cough came from the direction of Mom. She usually wasn't so obvious, but Max realized that maybe he'd not let her be as much a part as he could have. He'd been too busy getting it done.

He crossed his arms, feeling suddenly defensive. Not something he was used to. "Okay, you tell me."

"Traditional oak barrister book cases. Leather nail-head

furniture, probably maroon. Ponderous desks, heavy and dark. Old pictures, maybe oil paintings. All the rooms closed off, little rabbit warrens of space. No plans in place to upgrade as necessary for computer, Internet wireless, or whatever comes in the future."

"Rooms are closed off for client confidentiality."

"They don't have to always be closed off, they could have glass walls. There are shades that are stunning when pulled down or glass etchings to create privacy. Do you want to work in a dark cubby? Even if it's in a spacious room?"

5

MAX'S FROWN CARVED DEEPER INTO HIS FACE AS CARO LAID OUT the vision she thought he was seeing for his new space. She'd heard Mrs. Henderson's covered laugh but focused solely on Max.

This was a strategy that she always used. Before presenting the plans after her consults with the client, she memorized them so when she talked about the engineering or the aesthetics of the project she could study her client's face and body language. Engaged or rebuffed.

Max was not engaged. She knew she'd nailed his new office vision. It would have been stunning.

"You got four out of six," he said with a grudging tone.

"What did I get wrong?"

"The lack of high-tech stuff, I told you Margo was in on the planning of all of it and it should be golden."

Caro laughed, then sobered. Victory wasn't yet in reach. "Okay, so why keep the heavy old-style furniture and put up drywall to hide all this amazing brick?" She waved her arm around. "Old doesn't mean old fashioned."

"Exactly, just because the furniture is classic doesn't mean it's stodgy."

"Old and stodgy are two different concepts."

"Just listen for a minute, okay?"

Caro nodded and turned her full attention to listening and not prejudging. Hard, but doable.

"I want clients to walk through that door and know immediately that they are in a law firm that is successful, has longevity, and feels the part they expect."

She waited until she was sure he was done. Nothing more forthcoming. "So, it seems to me that you are defining what success means to other people."

"Perhaps, however, isn't everybody driven by success, and doesn't each vision of said success come with its own trappings?"

Caro nodded. "On some level I suppose that's true."

"Of course it is. Most people are driven by success."

"I don't think I'm driven by success, I think I'm driven by a challenge. And my goal is to take that challenge and make it as successful as possible. My client has a view of what they want their float or object to be, what vision they have of that year's parade theme, be it peace, happiness, or children's welfare and adoptions." Caro shrugged. "Whatever it is. My challenge, my job, is to interpret that idea in a way that is not only beautiful but functional. Something that makes people stop if only for a second and marvel at it or ponder the question the float or object is presenting." She knew she sounded overly earnest but it was all true—it's how she ran her life and her business, and as the two were braided together so tightly, the lines delineating the braid were nearly indistinguishable.

Geri stood, catching Caro's attention. "Max, ever since your father died you've been driven by the need to prove to everyone that you are the most successful person on the block. Even as a kid you wanted to be the best at everything you did. Dad tried to temper that and I've tried, but you're a grown man now, and sometimes I think you're an old man because you can't change your viewpoint. However, whatever you decide to do with the business in the building is fine by me."

She took a few steps toward Caro. "Caro, it's been an absolute pleasure meeting you. I like your vision, in fact I embrace your vision for the office, but it's Max's practice, so I bid you goodbye and good luck, and if you're still around, I'm having a dinner of homemade spaghetti and my favorite sauce on Wednesday, the day before Christmas Eve. I'd love to have a long talk over dinner about how you come up with your float ideas. Oh, and Max, if Caro is still speaking to you, you're invited as well." With that Geri got up, kissed Max on the cheek, and left the building without any drama whatever.

Max's mom's insight into her son sealed the knowledge that Caro was fighting a losing battle. She metaphorically took several steps back. Max hadn't asked her to design the space, he'd just asked her to simply read the plans and make sure what she saw corresponded with what was being done. She needed to remember that her thoughts about it being great didn't matter. *Stop it, it will be great. Maybe not in your eyes, but in Max's.* "Okay. I accept that my vision isn't your vision. Let me look at the project bible and check out the time lines."

CARO HAD MADE A COMPELLING ARGUMENT, AND AS A TRAINED attorney he never ignored those.

Could he take this leap of faith with his practice?

He drew a deep breath. "Can you sketch out the entry the way you envision it?"

"Of course."

Max was awed by the change in Caro with his simple

request. Her gray eyes lit up with excitement and the challenge ahead as she quickly searched the table for paper and pencils.

"I don't see any big paper. Do you mind if I use the back of one of the plans?"

"Go for it."

First, she quickly drew the outside of the building, leaving the door ajar. Stunned that she remembered so much detail in her short view of it, he was fascinated to watch it come alive under her fingers.

She moved over to the entry door, looked around for a few minutes, then headed back to the table.

Deftly drawing a large-scale front doorway, Caro drew him a view of what a client would see entering the office. He watched as, gripping the pencil, she sketched a space that blended old Boulder with a progressive law firm, melding the two so well that he easily visualized the glass conference room and offices, which she drew half shuttered. The front desk was modern and backed by panels of etched glass showing the iconic Boulder Flatirons.

With a few strokes of her pencil, he could see her plan for a sleek coffee and beverage station that rivaled any coffee shop around. A grouping of chairs looked comfortable and inviting. The staircase was featured to the left of the reception area.

Finally she put down her pencil. "You look. I'm going to eat my muffin."

"I don't need to look, I'm impressed. But I don't see how I can get this done in two weeks before I need to move in."

"The space isn't changing, just how we, I mean you, choose to enclose it. It can be done, or mostly done in two weeks. You and Margo can order furniture that isn't custom. How many associates do you have?"

Max was still stuck on the "we" she used. Once again, it struck him as right.

"Max?"

"Sorry, what? I was processing all you were saying."

"How many associates?"

"Two. Two secretaries, one paralegal. One receptionist. But we'll mostly likely be increasing staff."

"Okay."

She flipped through the plans, then pointed to ones showing the upstairs layout. "Are these their offices?"

He glanced at the blueprint. "Yes. The associates and paralegal offices are upstairs." He shifted back to the ground floor blueprints. "And these are the secretarial offices."

"So all the space is designed out. And the space is all functional and flows well. Can you give me a few hours to make some calls to suppliers? Assuming of course that you're serious."

Was he? Suddenly he worried he was moving way too fast and was making a mistake. He usually examined a situation from all angles. Yet Caro and her vision appealed to him. He wanted to agree. Dare he take that chance?

6

No, it was too much. Caro was right. Her vision and his didn't match.

His new office wasn't going to be stodgy. It was traditional. The computers made it modern.

And it would all take too much time, regardless of what she said. Not to mention he was sure it was going to cost a whole heck of a lot more. And perhaps the added expense of an elevator.

He saw the excitement fade from Caro's gray eyes as he formulated what to say.

"Hey, it's okay. We're not on the same page, and I'm not offended at all. After the framing is completed and the electrical is installed, I want to look at the plans and make sure they were followed before the electrical inspection is made. Just so we don't have to fix something and deal with that delay."

"You're still willing to take it on?"

"Sure, it gives me something to do. Besides knit, you know? And I promised both my parents and Brice that I wouldn't work on Forever Young stuff—"

"Forever Young?"

"The name of my company. A play on my last name."

"Right, now I remember Brice mentioning it."

"Anyway they think I needed a break. But I'll be happy to get home after the holiday and dig into work. So yeah, call me."

She pulled down her knitted cap and rewrapped her muffler around her neck as she headed for the door.

"Wait, I'll drive you back."

Hand on the door knob, she turned around. "No, really. It's a short walk and the fresh air will be great. Give your mom my regrets for dinner, okay? She's a pretty awesome woman. And pasta is one of my favorite foods."

Max stood still as the door closed behind Caro. He noticed she didn't say, "Maybe another time." And damn if confusion, an emotion he had little experience with, didn't boil up and swirl through him in a miasma of color. Was he wrong? Was he stodgy? Or was Caro too bright, bohemian, and carefree?

Maybe she's everything you aren't. Isn't that why you're attracted to her?

He snatched up the plans she'd drawn, carefully locked the office door behind him, got into his Porsche and headed up a snow-packed Broadway to his old office at a crawl.

Old? Where did that thought come from.

Caro.

IT WASN'T A LONG WALK BACK TO THE BOULDERADO, AND THE sunshine made it feel warmer even if it wasn't raising the bubble on the thermometer. Caro had little desire to go back to the hotel, and walking would work out her frustration. She wasn't mad at Max, and maybe frustration was too big a word. Disappointed that he was not taking this step to make his building and thus the image of his practice more exciting. Even more upscale.

Disappointment was part of her biz. Sometimes people just didn't like a design. No hard feelings, and she would help Max as much as she could if he indeed did call again.

She passed a yarn store that was just opening. Backtracking a few feet, she entered, and immediately her tension melted as the subtle earthiness of wool yarn blended with the richness of coffee and the tang of cinnamon and cloves enveloped her. Caro was in heaven.

"Can I help you find anything?" a soft voice from her left inquired.

Still a bit snowblinded, Caro squinted and finally focused on a diminutive woman, her long gray hair piled in a bun on top of her head and held in place by what looked like white lacquered chopsticks.

"Hello. It's my first time in your shop. It's lovely. I live in Pasadena, and can you move your shop there?"

A hearty chuckle answered her question. "Welcome, and no, but I can give you names of some similar shops there that you may enjoy."

"I'd love that. Do you stock vicuña wool?"

"Actually, I have a few skeins left. Follow me."

Caro blinked twice at the price and then bought enough for mittens, a couple of scarves and maybe a hat. "Thank you. I'm here until after Christmas, so I'll stop back in and pick up those names if you don't mind."

"We'll close early on Christmas Eve and be closed until Monday, but I'll gather those names for you and have them here."

Caro left the shop, the bag of yarn clutched tightly, and suddenly realized one reason Max was concerned about changing the plans. Christmas Eve would be a partial work day, and she'd bet the contractors wouldn't be back until Monday. Then there would be another short work week with New Year's.

Immediately the need to call him hit her. She looked up the number for Henderson, Stout and Henderson and reached their answering machine. Of course, it was Sunday.

"Max, it's Caro. I didn't have your cell number but call me back anytime if you want. I just ran through the shortened weeks in my mind, realizing how crunched your timetable is. I'll help however I can."

It was the best near-apology she could make.

Upstairs in her hotel room, Caro grabbed her needles and headed back to the lobby. Sitting alone didn't appeal to her at all, but starting work with the vicuña wool did.

Settling in the deep armchair, needles at the ready, she paused as she visualized knitting something for Max—not the vicuña, but something soft. Images filled her mind, but the color of the muffler and gloves completely escaped her. Black was boring, brown too ordinary, red too bold ... or maybe not. Maybe that's exactly what he needed.

Once she figured it out, she could easily get what she required at the knitting shop right around the corner. Deciding on Max's color was going to be the issue.

But then, knitting anything for Max might be a moot point. Would he call her, or was their brief time together over?

7

"ARE YOU CRAZY?" MARGO DEMANDED AS SHE LOOKED AT THE sketches Max laid out on the conference table.

"I know. That's why I haven't agreed to make the changes. Yet."

"Who is she that'd you even think of making such radical changes?"

"Brice's sister. An engineer and the owner of Forever Young, a float-designing and building company in California."

"Those are her creds for this job?"

Max didn't like Margo's attacking attitude at all. "Yeah, they're more than good enough. I brought the drawing here because I wanted to see how our furniture would fit in with her vision."

"Why are you listening to her?"

"Why the third degree?" Max questioned in a deceptively mild voice, not particularly liking her tone.

"Because I like her vision. It's modern, yet old. It shows a progressive attitude."

Max sat down, stunned. Was he the only one who was stuck in the rut?

"But I still want to keep Dad's old desk."

Margo left and returned in a few minutes with two cups of coffee and a phone number. "The phone message light was on." She put a sticky note in front of him. "That number is your float builder's."

"Caro?"

"I'd like to meet her. Why don't you pick her up and bring her back. I've got a few more points to cover before the trial tomorrow, so I'll be here for at least another couple of hours."

A knock sounded on the door.

Margo turned on the monitor sitting on Max's desk. They all had one as they worked late and locked up the office after hours. But sometimes a client needed to see them outside of office hours.

The view of the front door showed him a bundled-up woman with fiery hair peeking out from beneath her cap. "Caro?"

"Your float builder is here?"

"God, she must be freezing." Max said as he hurried from his office to the vestibule and opened the door.

"Get in here, are you crazy?" he asked, well aware of the concern lacing his voice. Didn't matter, it was bloody cold outside.

"Hi to you too. And not too crazy—there are all sorts of places open to get warm or coffee. But with that hill climb, I didn't have a chance to get cold, and there is a Starbucks just down the street, you know." Caro held up her cup for emphasis.

"Yes, I know, but you're still crazy." And was rewarded with a brilliant smile before she turned to Margo.

"Hi, I'm Caroline Young. I'm guessing you're Margo Stout?" Caro stepped around Max.

"I am. Good guess. Max was just talking about picking you up and bringing you back to meet me."

Max folded his arms and leaned against the wall. Margo still had her full attorney persona going. He wondered why, especially if she liked Caro's ideas.

He intercepted Caro's questioning glance and nodded his affirmation of Margo's declaration.

"Why?"

"Because I wanted to talk to you about your ideas."

"Max pretty much nixed them." Caro turned to him. "Right?"

He nodded.

Margo shook her head. "Yes, he told me. So why did you come up here in near-zero weather?"

Caro shrugged and unwound her knitted scarf. "Honestly? I was sitting in the hotel, knitting—" she paused to laugh at Margo's raised brows. "Anyway, instead of it calming me as it usually does, I was antsy. Max had described the Hill and it sounded interesting and my phone GPS said it wasn't far, so I headed out. When I saw lights on in here I decided to stop and look at the furniture Max said was going in the new space to see if I was interpreting Debra's floor plan correctly."

Max said nothing for fear his admiration for Caro would come bursting through. Which wasn't something he wanted to share with the world yet. For not only was he amazingly pleased to see her again, he was impressed with her ability to be friendly under Margo's third degree and the fact that she was being incredibly conscientious about the responsibility she'd willingly undertaken with his office.

Caro sipped her coffee as they both apparently waited for Margo's reply.

USUALLY CARO COULD READ PEOPLE PRETTY DARN WELL, BUT Margo was an enigma. Did the woman dislike her? Or was Caro competition of some sort? She had absolutely no idea, except that it would be easier all around if Margo at least wasn't so antagonistic toward her.

"So why couldn't you convince Max that your ideas are spot on and exactly what Henderson, Stout and Henderson needs for the future?"

Caro nearly let her jaw drop at Margo's change in attitude. Even Max straightened against the wall in surprise. "I tried, I honestly tried. He's just a bit stubborn."

Margo's laugh rang out. She nodded sagely. "That's the kindest description I can think of. Old school, regimented, and stuck in a rut."

"Oh, not that bad, surely?" Caro tried hard to contain her laugh, but failed completely.

"Hey, I'm right here, you know," Max said.

"But he's a damned fine attorney and good mentor."

"Thank you, I think."

Margo curtsied. "Seriously, Caro, how much time would the changes take?"

Caro moved around the room, inspecting the receptionist's desk, and then glanced at the furniture in the lobby. As she'd guessed, maroon leather and nailhead furniture filled the area and tall barrister bookcases lined the wall

She took a breath and released it. "The biggest thing is going to be getting in the glass for the partitions and the furniture that works. For the price that we, er, you want to pay."

Caro spied an amazing photograph of the Boulder Flatirons on the wall in the lobby. "Wow, that photo is brilliant. I had imagined something like that etched into the glass behind the receptionist's desk. Now we could use this image on the glass and hang the photo opposite it."

"Thank you."

Caro looked at Margo. "You took that picture?"

"Yes."

"You're very talented."

"Light is everything in photography."

"As it is in space designing. It would be stunning."

She was now dying to see Max's office. She expected heavy oak furniture and more of those barrister bookcases. "Can you give me a second to look at your office?" she asked, glancing at Max.

"Remember I said you nailed four out of six?"

She moved to the door Max held open and peeked in. "Seriously? Your desk is the sixth? Shockingly modern."

Max smiled. "Thought you'd like it. It's actually very functional."

"So why balk at the rest? It's not like you don't appreciate modern."

"I need the office up and running right after the New Year. One issue is getting everything ordered. And two, you're leaving next week before it can all be done."

8

CARO'S HEARTBEAT SPED UP AT THE SUDDEN HEAT IN HIS NAVY EYES and the way his voice grew husky when he paused and said "you're." This was not personal, she told herself. But it was a lie. Their relationship had just shifted a degree or two and become just that.

Personal.

The world receded, holding just them.

Max took a step toward her and she leaned forward.

"Ahem. I think I'll go back to my office and do my last bit of prep," Margo said.

Caro barely registered the words until she saw Max take a step back. Damn, what was wrong with her that she lost all sense of place and time?

"Good idea. But before you go, Margo, I believe the right way to handle the office is to use Caro's plan."

"Max, I knew you were smart," Margo tossed over her shoulder and then left them alone in the lobby of the office.

Swallowing twice, Caro thought her voice was steady enough not to betray her. "You're serious? Because we have some decisions to make."

"Yes. The rough part is that I have client appointments I have to take in between all this. I lightened my load as much as possible, but ..."

"That's fine. I'll work up the products and prices. Make some calls, then we can meet up late Monday and go over everything. Does that work?"

At his nod, she continued. "Meanwhile, tell me what you think should move to the new office, and I'll tell you if I agree."

Max opened then shut his mouth.

She was proud of him. "I'm kidding of course. You, Margo, and your staff choose and make a list of what is necessary for them. The receptionist's desk and seating area though will all be new. As will the coffee station and conference room. We may have to wait a bit for the desk to be made, so we can use what you have here."

"You're the boss—"

"You're the client. You do have final say."

"Then can I ask you to stay until it's done?"

CARO DIDN'T ANSWER RIGHT AWAY, AND MAX SAW INDECISION WAR with something, possibly regret, in her eyes and understood it.

He knew this was a short association from the start and had no place to go. His practice was here in Boulder, and he couldn't move to California. Her business and warehouse were there.

So that left them with little to work with except the time they had now. *Enjoy your time with her. Brice is here, you're here, maybe she'll visit more often. Maybe you can make her want to visit more often.*

"Max?"

He focused on her and wasn't encouraged by her furrowed brow. "I'm sensing my request was too much?"

Caro lifted her shoulders in a mini shrug. "I can't promise to stay past Friday the first. There won't be any work done on your office from late Thursday to Monday anyway. I have a client meeting on Monday I have to prepare for, so I need to be back Friday early enough to get started on the details of the presentation."

Now he saw regret, and hoped it meant she was sorry she had to leave.

"So, will you stay until then?"

"Yes."

Yes, he fist-pumped, then swept her against his chest in a hug. Her arms crept around him and she looked up at him.

He wasn't about to resist the invitation and captured her lips in a kiss he hoped she wouldn't refuse.

She didn't. Opening her lips slightly, she nibbled his bottom lip. He cupped her cheek and deepened their kiss, and the world felt right.

His plan for enjoying their time together suddenly became more important. Kissing usually meant passion, but this was more. This was like sharing a soul.

Max wasn't sure if Caro felt the same, but somehow, in some totally irrational, emotional way, far from being logical, he was sure she did.

Lifting his head the merest amount he gazed into Caro's eyes and saw wonder.

She didn't step away, thankfully. She did grin.

"Okay, that's going to make concentrating on finding furniture and glass panels pretty damn hard. And I have dinner with my folks tonight, which I begged off from last night. Do you want to come along?"

Laughter rumbled in his chest. "Yes, I want to come, but I'll pass only because you're way too distracting. Let's make this list of items to keep. I'm starving and thought we could grab soup and a sandwich at Innisfree, and then I'll drive you back to the hotel."

The list took very little time as each staff member would be packing up their own stuff during the coming week.

The coffee shop was hot and steamy, and they found places at the counter facing the street. It wasn't crowded, but it was busy.

Each brush of Caro's hand next to his, or the wondering glances she gave him, nearly had him repeating the kiss they'd just shared. He let loose a sigh.

"Me too," Caro said softly.

Leaving the café, Caro stopped and looked across the block to the campus of the University of Colorado. "Brice told me there is a bridge over a pond, not far from the Hill. Can we walk there?"

"Varsity Pond. It's this way." He led the way past the rural Italian renaissance-style buildings of Colorado sandstone topped with red tile roofs, to the stone bridge over the pond.

"You know what a movie buff Brice is—"

"Insane is the better word."

"Well, then maybe I shouldn't tell you this, but I knew something he didn't." He smiled at her, hoping the suspense would get to her.

He waited patiently, looking at the sky, the pond, at her.

"Okay, spill it."

He grinned. "The Glenn Miller Story was filmed right here. And once back at the studio, although they had to recreate the bridge and reshoot back in Hollywood because of technical problems, Jimmy Stewart and June Allyson were standing where we are now." Max widened his arms to embrace the entire scene in front of them and got the response from Caro he'd hoped for.

She snuggled up against him, and they slowly crossed the bridge arm in arm.

He was as warm as could be, but he noticed Caro shivered a bit.

"Time to head back. We'll come here again some warm spring day."

"That's a promise I'll keep you to."

He smiled down at her because she'd just admitted she would be returning to Boulder. Maybe he *was* growing on her.

On the drive back to the hotel, Max stopped at a red light and reached for her hand, clasping it, then raised it to his lips and kissed her fingers.

The contact was nearly as intense as the kiss they'd shared a few hours ago. Maybe it was the fact that time was short, and every emotion was amplified.

NOW THAT THE MAIN ROADS WERE PLOWED, THE DRIVE BACK TO her hotel was way too short. For the entire drive Caro kept her eyes on Max, not the scenery.

Oh, Lordy, she had it bad. And that scared her.

Forcing herself to recall that she only had ten, maybe eleven more days here allowed her to simply enjoy. No commitments, no future in Boulder.

Couldn't be any other way.

Still, when they reached the Boulderado, Caro hated for their day together to end. She consoled herself with the thought that they'd be in contact soon, like tomorrow.

And she had a lot of work in front of her. This was going to be a project of the heart.

Stop it. That sounds way too serious. You can't let it be.

Max got out and opened her door. Caro swung her feet out, then stopped. "Wait. I have to get the bible."

"Excuse me?"

"The project bible. All project designers use one. It was on the big table next to the plans. Debra left it there, knowing someone would use it if necessary. I need it, but I'm supposed to meet my parents in ten minutes."

"Okay, I'll get it and leave it at the desk, will that be okay?"

Caro thought for a second, "I can't afford to lose it. Can you get it, and I'll wait for you right here?"

"Sure. I didn't realize it was that important."

"It's everything from phone numbers to order numbers. Pictures to fabric swatches."

"Okay but wait inside. I'll see you in less than ten."

"Thank you, Max," Looking around swiftly and not seeing anyone, she bussed his cheek with a kiss.

A smile creased his face and lit his eyes as he got back into the Porsche SUV.

She floated into the hotel but stayed near the door to watch for his return. *Stop it, you have a family gig next and then you have a lot of online work to do.*

She swiftly made mental lists of the manufacturers she knew that might have what she needed. Once back at the hotel, she'd text Bri, her go-to facilitator for suppliers, and have her search contacts in the Boulder-Denver area. Then she'd check the project bible and find out who was making the windows.

Darn, she'd totally forgotten to ask Margo about the elevator. She'd jot it down and dig in on that with Max tomorrow.

Speaking of the man, he drove up and double-parked. She ran out to meet him and took the book he handed out the window along with a set of keys. "You'll need these for the office. Have fun with your folks. Talk to you tomorrow. Sweet dreams."

A crowd of people entered the hotel as she leaned in the car's window. She didn't really want spectators, neither did she want him to leave with a kiss. "I won't hit the sack until well into the early morning, but when I do, I'll dream—" she cleared her voice of its sudden huskiness, "—of you." She finished on a whisper and quickly bussed him on the lips.

And left him speechless.

9

MONDAY MORNING CAME EARLY, BUT CARO HAD BEEN RARING TO go. What little sleep she did get was filled with dreams of Max, and she couldn't wait to see him today.

She'd texted him before she headed out to the office so that he'd be sure to let the framers know there were revisions to the plans and that she'd be there to direct them.

Now they were framing the walls for the closets and file rooms upstairs. She'd decided to nix the dry wall up there, rationalizing that glass cubicles would allow the upstairs to take advantage of passive solar.

Electrical power to all the glass offices would be core-drilled in the floor and run through the channels beneath the panel dividers, making it look seamless. Expensive, but worth it.

The only drywall was going to be in the closets and file rooms. And that was plenty.

She was expecting calls from Bri, her go-to facilitator for suppliers, and from a couple of vendors and the electrical inspector confirming the inspection date. Her stomach rumbled and she checked the time on her phone. Breakfast was over six hours ago.

As she searched the Internet for a restaurant that would deliver, her phone rang. "Caroline Young speaking."

"Are you hungry?"

Hearing Max's voice, she smiled. "Starving."

"Good, look to your right."

Caro turned to find Max, phone to his ear, standing in the doorway, his other hand holding bags of something that smelled divine. Seeing him created another craving—for something less substantial but more filling.

A kiss from him.

Tucking his phone into his jacket pocket, he headed straight toward her, stopped, looked around quickly, then pulled her against him with his free arm.

Though he was grinning, his eyes smoldered with undeniable heat. And lord knew, she felt the same flush of desire. His mouth covered hers, and Caro simply let her bones melt as she leaned against him.

They heard steps on the staircase and pulled apart. Drat.

"Hey, Mister Henderson." A cheerful man with Boulder Stud and Framing embroidered on his white shirt greeted Max, then turned to Caro. "Ms. Young, upstairs is nearly done, but the electrician asked me to tell you that he has a problem with pulling wire at the stairs junction."

Caro intercepted Max's slight nod. "Show me," she requested, and followed the framing contractor back up the stairs.

Back in less than five minutes, she found Max had created a feast from the bags. Sushi and noodle soup from Hapa, decadent-looking chocolate for dessert.

"Oh, I love Hapa sushi," Caro said.

"I wasn't really a sushi lover until Brice and Jen introduced me to Hapa. Now I'm hooked," Max replied.

"Yeah, they took me there on my first visit to Boulder."

"Too bad I didn't get to meet you then."

Caro put down her sushi roll and stared at him. "I was only in town for a few days each time I visited."

"That's a few days I could have seen you, even if for only a few minutes. I know you were busy here. Jennifer said you're a whirlwind when you work."

His words created a flurry of contrary emotions. She didn't do relationships. She had friends, partied and chatted and once in a great while confided in them. But relationships meant losing her hard-fought independence. Something she'd sought since she was old enough to understand that life in Kansas wasn't all there was to *life*.

She'd been painted a rebel, or a wild child, because she pushed back. It was in her nature. And as she'd told Max, her teachers didn't appreciate her questioning them. So her answer was to strike out on her own, even as a teen.

She went solo.

Her parents' marriage was a good role model for a healthy and loving relationship. And Caro had taken psychology in college and understood the difference between independent and interdependence in a relationship.

The thought of a relationship and the effort needed to make it succeed sounded like too much work. Add the needs of her business and well ...

Yet, Max brought out a yearning in her to be part of something more than just herself. She enjoyed being around him, more than enjoyed. Damn, she dreamed of him last night and couldn't wait to see him today. Yet Max's simple observation had her tied up with apprehension.

You can't have it both ways.

Caro couldn't answer his lovely and fear-inducing comment. She had no idea what to say.

As if Max could tell he'd said too much, he tucked into his

meal and focused on eating. And Caro instantly missed the connection.

When she touched his hand, he looked swiftly at her. Caro met his gaze. "Even though I don't and can't live here, I can visit. I will visit."

He cocked his head and stared at her wordlessly. She couldn't look away and yet she knew what she'd just said wasn't enough for him.

She decided it was time to change the subject. "Okay, want a rundown on what's happening? I have some great news."

At his single nod, she summoned up enthusiasm and summarized the new work list. "And the staircase is being delivered tomorrow and installed Wednesday after the drywallers are done with their curtailed work. Paint Thursday and, as it's Christmas Eve, they should be done by the afternoon. No more work until Monday, when the panels and furniture and coffee machines with their cabinets will be delivered through Wednesday next week. The biggie is the inspection, but your electrician pretty much guaranteed me that the city would get it done in time. I'm just waiting for their phone call to confirm."

"Seriously? You got all that done?"

"I had help and unbelievable luck. A huge petroleum company opened a new Denver office and leased five floors in some big new tower downtown. The home office downsized the operation before the furniture installation was complete. Get this, they have a warehouse full of gorgeous glass panels and some incredible furniture that I'm going to look at tomorrow. The best part? I can get it at liquidation prices.

"And I've arranged for a triptych of glass panels hanging from the ceiling to go behind the receptionist's desk with the same view as the picture of the Flatirons that Margo took. It will be stunning." She didn't tell him about the special surprise she had for him.

Even if she wouldn't be here to give it to him on his first day in the new office. After all, she hadn't promised to stay past Friday, the first. That was stretching her timetable as far as possible.

Caro had enlisted Margo's help to reprint and enlarge the photo of his dad and Margo's that she'd spied on the wall in Max's office. Max could hang it in his office. It was going to be double-sided and she'd arranged for some special hanging brackets to work with the glass-paneled walls.

~

MAX HEARD ALL CARO'S PLANS AND NODDED APPROPRIATELY, while his mind churned on her last words, "Even though I don't and can't live here, I can visit. I will visit."

He wasn't sure why it bothered him so much that she was treating "them" in such a cavalier way. It's not like he didn't know her company and life were in California.

Fool, it's because she's something you're not and it completely intrigues you. You moved beyond mere interest in her when you kissed her.

Caro had created a chink in his armor. And though she'd returned his kisses with a passion that had given him a sense that she was falling for him as he was for her, apparently that wasn't the case.

Can't you just enjoy the time with her and not make a big deal out of it?

"Max?"

He focused back on her. "What?"

"You were on another planet."

"Yeah, that happens sometimes when a thought comes up about a case."

Disappointment flickered in her eyes and he instantly hated himself. What a chicken he was turning into.

"I understand. Anyway, Debra picked a gorgeous gray and brown Berber for the carpets and I think we should keep it. It's perfect."

"Go for it." His phone buzzed and he realized it was time to head back to the old office and meet with an estate client.

"I've got an appointment in a bit. Listen, do you want to have dinner tonight?"

He braved her intense look.

"Are you sure you want to? You don't need to," she said, her voice hesitant.

"Oh, yes I do." Damn, that wasn't supposed to slip out. But it was worth it to see her gray eyes light up.

"Then yes. I'll text you when I leave here. Then give me forty-five minutes to clean off the dust."

"Okay if I grill steaks?"

"In this weather?"

"I grill in any weather."

"Then you're on. I love a great steak."

"Then I'm your man." Damn, he did it again. "Oh, and Mom extends her invite for Wednesday pasta night to the whole Young clan."

"Wow, that's nice of her. I'm sure Mom and Dad will love meeting her. Have Brice and Jen met her?"

"Many times. Have you heard from them?"

"Yeah, they're back and at work. Didn't even have time to chat much, but we'll catch up at your mom's place."

"Great. Gotta run." He got up and began to stuff the remnants of their lunch back into the sacks.

"Don't worry, I'll clean up." Caro looked at him uncertainly, checked the staircase, and back at him. "Got a second for a goodbye kiss to hold me over until dinner?"

An amazing relief flooded through him. *Remember, enjoy the moments.*

In answer, he pulled her close and captured her lips, drawing out the kiss as long as he could.

"By the way, did you dream of me last night?" he asked when he came up for air.

"What do you think?"

10

CARO WAITED FOR MAX IN THE LOBBY OF THE BOULDERADO HOTEL near the massive Christmas tree, leaning on the black grand piano RJ was playing. When he finished his piece, she moved closer and bussed him on the cheek.

"How are you doing, Caro?"

"Max is keeping me very busy. Did you know I was filling in for his designer, who's sick?"

"I heard. And that you have some great new plans."

How did he know?

"Hey, you want to play?" he asked before starting a new set.

She grimaced. "Um, no. I'm way rusty and believe it or not, while I can be crazy in public, performing is totally a nerve wrecker."

RJ tilted his head slightly to look behind her and smiled.

"Now that I don't believe." Max's deep voice sounded at her shoulder.

Her knees turned to quivering masses of cartilage. "It's true," she said. "As you know, Brice can perform anywhere. But me, I'm a background person."

"Again, impossible to believe. RJ, what are your plans for Wednesday night?" Max asked.

"Play until six, then off until Sunday. Got a relief player, a kid from CU."

"Mom is having a big dinner, and we'd love to have you. Margo is coming."

Caro saw RJ's eyes light up.

"Sure, I'd love to. Will there be enough room?"

"You know Mom. Always."

"Okay, see you after six." RJ played a jazzy version of "The Christmas Song."

As Caro slid on her jacket and tucked her arm into Max's, she heard people starting to sing "Chestnuts roasting on an open fire."

"Chestnuts are great, but I'm starving for steak."

"Then let's get you fed. The Porsche is out front in the dropoff zone."

As they drove off, Caro enjoyed the fairy lights entwined in the pine garlands that festooned the balconies on the upper floors of the hotel. And to keep the holiday mood, Max had Christmas songs on the stereo. They turned back onto Broadway, and Caro realized the entire downtown Pearl Street Mall was decorated in lights and banners. The houses and condos lining the broad street seemed to carry on the bright holiday theme.

"All this certainly makes me want a snowy Christmas every year. The lights are beautiful and happy."

"I can't wait to show you the Flagstaff Star from my deck. And have you seen Annie's house?"

"Nope, heard about it though. Is she leaving it lit while they're on their honeymoon?"

"Nothing will ever convince her not to have her Christmas lights shine."

"Then maybe we can drive by sometime before I leave."

"Sure, I'd love to show it to you."

It was only a few more blocks, then up the steep hill and into the cul-de-sac where he lived.

Caro caught a glimpse of his house before he pulled into his massive three-car garage. The house looked as big as Jen's but was more sleek and modern with pale stucco walls, dark brown trim and a bluestone walkway.

Max opened her car door and then the door into his house. "Welcome to my home," he said as he swept his arm before her.

The timbre of his voice dropped a notch, his words almost a caress. Caro ached for his hands on her skin in the touch his voice promised.

Damn if she wasn't in trouble—and she hadn't even taken off her coat yet.

Max left Caro on his deck, the heaters turned on high, and returned to his kitchen to pour the cabernet he'd left open to breathe. He pulled the steaks out of the fridge to let them warm up a bit before he ignited the grill. On the way back to Caro, he turned on the fireplace.

He slid the door open and watched her for a moment as she stood still, her profile illuminated by the indoor lights as she stood at the railing looking toward the mountains.

"Here you go." He held out a glass.

Caro turned and he was stunned by the awe gleaming in her eyes. "You didn't tell me the star was magical."

"Is it?"

She took her glass, then clinked it against his. "Here's to the magic of the season."

He looked at the star and back at her, deciding that indeed, maybe the star was magical. "To the star, and to you, who believes in its magic."

"I noticed you don't have a tree up."

"No, I spend Christmas day at Mom's and so use hers."

"Annie wouldn't approve."

Max chuckled. "I've had a series of lectures already. Even Jen is on my case. So next year I better get in gear, or else."

"Or else what?"

"They've withheld the penalty, but the verdict would be guilty."

She smiled and took another sip of her cabernet. "This is really good wine, far beyond what I can afford."

"Actually, probably not. It's all in the decanting. I'll share my secret with you. Want to come in while I get everything ready?"

"Sure, I want to help."

Max led the way, sensing that she'd stopped, and he turned to see why. She stood at the kitchen door, bug-eyed.

"Do you really use this—" she hesitated, then apparently found the word—"chef's kitchen, or is it to wow people?"

"You've got some issues with the trapping of success, or at least my trappings, don't you?" He said it lightly but was confused by her sudden change of attitude. "Of course I use it. Mom taught me how to cook when I was old enough to safely handle a knife. Once you get to know her better, you'll see that she believes in everyone holding their own. Only Dad got away with not doing the dishes, but he made a mean omelet."

Caro nodded, took off her coat, and hung it on one of the tall, high-backed stools lined up along the kitchen's island.

"I'm sorry. That was pure reaction and not fair at all. It's just that this is all so grand compared to my Airstream."

"And functional. I had it designed so I could cook. And, Caro, I warn you, Mom's kitchen has this beat by miles."

"I'd take it all back if I could. Forgive me?"

"Of course." He picked up his wine glass and touched it lightly to hers.

Caro made the salad as he checked the progress of the baking potatoes. After his client meeting, he'd run to the butcher's, swung by the market, and then sped home.

In less than thirty minutes, they were seated at his dining room table, and Caro took her first bite.

"Oh my, this is probably the best steak I've eaten, ever."

"I bet you say that to all your dates who fix you dinner."

She smiled, but he glimpsed an emotion in her eyes that belied her smile. It took a moment until he realized it was loneliness. That tore at him. How on earth could anybody as fun and lively as Caro not have a cadre of friends to call upon.

"Nope, just you. I don't really have the time to date. In fact, this vacation is the longest stretch of non-work I've had since I started Forever Young."

"And I'm making you work."

"I volunteered."

He smiled at her defiant tone. "I didn't have time to date either with college, law school, taking on and then building the practice. Even now dates are pretty rare."

Now her smile twinkled in her eyes as well. "Aren't we the pair?"

He lifted his glass in an agreeing toast, and for the next little while they ate in companionable silence.

Dessert was Ethiopian coffee and a thick slice of tiramisu.

"The deck heater is still on—would you like to finish coffee out there?"

"I'd love to. I can't get enough of the star."

And what about me?

He shook off the useless emotion, reminding himself to enjoy the moments.

Yet, Caro's enthusiasm reminded him that she was such an

open spirit. Something he wanted in his life. She embraced new adventures easily. Too bad she was deeply rooted in California, and the adventure of moving wasn't in her playbook.

Max stifled his sigh and helped Caro with her jacket, then watched as she wrapped a green muffler around her neck. He pulled on his coat and half gloves and slid the deck door open.

She leaned against the railing. "This is a view I could get used to. I'd love to see it in the summer. But the star at this time of year brings hope."

"That's interesting. That's what Annie says."

"She's an amazing woman."

"As you are. And we can arrange a summer viewing whenever you're here."

She turned to face him. He saw the uncertainty in her gaze and hated it. "No pressure, Caro, just an open invitation."

Caro's stare immediately turned impish, replacing that serious one. She took his coffee cup and, with her own, placed them on the glass table near them.

The next instant, her arms were around him, and she laid her cheek on his chest. "Thank you."

"For?"

"This moment. Your belief in me and ..."

She didn't finish. Instead of pressuring her, he tipped up her chin and bent to capture her lips in a searing kiss. Feeling her soft mouth give under his, he wanted her to believe in him. That he was worth thinking seriously about.

Heck, he wanted to scoop her up and carry her to the bedroom.

11

SHE'D ACCOMPLISHED SO MUCH IN TWO DAYS, AND YET CARO acknowledged the impatience coursing through her. She checked her phone more often today than she had in the previous days in Boulder combined.

Her morning trip to Denver and the warehouse holding the furniture and the glass panel systems had been an incredible success. Everything had been invoiced and the contract was waiting in her email folder by the time she'd returned to Boulder. She couldn't wait to tell Max the good news and find out about delivery dates from the company she'd hired to move everything from Denver to his new office.

Checking the phone yet again, and seeing nothing, Caro shook the phone in frustration and laid it down with less than her usual care.

Bing. Grabbing it up at the sound of a text, Caro found a message from exactly the person she'd been waiting for, Max.

Are you back? Sorry I can't make dinner, issues all over the place. Forgive me?

Yes of course, she typed quickly. *Fantastic find in warehouse. I'll miss seeing you.*

She hit the send button before she could change her mind about the last line.

Me too.

Caro smiled at his last text. Her impatience fled and her heart lightened. Life was good.

Another bing. She grabbed the phone quickly to find a text from her mom asking whether she'd eaten. Texting back that she hadn't yet had lunch, she waited a moment and sure enough, her mom said she'd be there in a bit, bringing food with her.

Over brioche sandwiches filled with rich ham and Gouda cheese, Caro showed her the plans for Max' office, both old and new.

"Pretty big undertaking."

Caro knew immediately that her mom was holding back. "Yes, it is a significant change and at the same time isn't. What bothers you about it, Mom?"

"Your plans are brilliant, and it will make this whole office shine, but what if—"

"Spit it out." Caro looked down at the sandwich in her hand and put it back on the butcher paper wrapper, then stared at her mom.

"You said you and Margo needed to convince him—what if he regrets going along with this. You are a strong personality to say no to."

"Mom, you say that as if it's a bad thing. Honest, we didn't twist his arm." *Much.* "Maximillian Henderson III is well aware of what he's doing. Once he's set on something I don't think he revisits the decision. And this will give him the essence of success he craves, with old Boulder and modern Boulder all in one glance."

"You seem to have him pretty well sized up. I know Jen and Brice think the world of him."

"Are you by any chance matchmaking?"

Her mother met her gaze with a steady one. And much to Caro's surprise, she was the one who looked away first. Then she felt her mother's fingers wrap around her hand and squeeze gently.

"No, honey, I'm not. I learned when you were in high school that you absolutely had a mind of your own about, well, about everything."

"And that's a bad thing?"

"Absolutely not. If you didn't know what you wanted you'd never have been able to create Forever Young and make it into the successful company you have in such short order. It's just that I, we, all of us, worry that you're becoming too focused on work and not allowing others to share your life."

"Mom, I don't think of it as focus. I think it's just that I'm in control—I take all the chances and I take all the heat if there is any."

"Yet you won't chance your heart."

"Then I'm not in control. I'm suddenly a couple. I don't want to be dependent on someone else for my happiness."

Laughter burst from her mother's lips. "You say that as if it's a bad thing. It's not. Being a couple doesn't mean co-joined at the hip. It means having someone there, perhaps to bounce ideas off. To build a life together.

"Honey, I know you had to leave Kansas just as Brice did. And I know you don't understand why Dad and I waited to marry until his business was steady enough to provide for us. We didn't want to take a chance of raising a young family and having a farm fail. We wanted several ways of being secure in a small town that saw wealth when the crops came in and desperation when they didn't. I know you think Dad and I were cheap—"

"Mom, now I know you were being frugal, just in case." Her

words brought a smile to her beloved mother's face. They rarely had time for talks like this. *Be honest, Caro, you rarely made the time.*

"Yes, just in case. And that's probably something that will never change. But that still doesn't take away what I'm saying about building a relationship that works for you both."

With that her mom gathered all the meal wrappings and stuffed them back in the sack she'd brought them in.

"See you later, honey."

Her mom was halfway out the door when a thought hit Caro. "Mom, wait."

She turned around with an eyebrow raised.

"What color do you think Max is?"

"Are you knitting him something?"

"Not yet."

"And you can't figure it out?"

"Nope."

"That's a first. Let me think on it. But frankly, you'll come to it. You always do." With that she closed the door behind her.

I'm not so sure this time, Mom. Not this time.

12

CARO ARRIVED AT MAX'S OFFICE BEFORE THE SUN WAS UP, LONG before the drywallers arrived. She'd left the heat on, needing the space to be warm for the drywall mud to cure quickly.

Even though the amount of dry-walling to be done had been radically reduced, there were still closets, file rooms, and storage spaces that needed to be done.

Additionally, she needed to check one more time that everything was right with the electrical and the footprint of the offices and windows. As she'd not been in the planning stages for this, double, even triple checking eased the nervousness in her gut.

She wanted this to be perfect for Max. Sure, things happened during a renovation, but minimizing the possibilities was vital. Just as she'd done for the wedding and for her floats.

And your life.

Where did that thought come from? She shook her head and went to work. After she'd measured the file rooms and the storage rooms, she headed back downstairs to check on the closets, electrical, and utility rooms.

All seemed right, yet nerves hit.

"Wow, you beat me here."

She let loose a small shriek and, hand to chest, turned to face the man behind the voice she'd missed so much yesterday. "Don't do that. I just lost a year off my life."

Max pulled her into his arms. "Let's see if I can get it back for you."

He nibbled her lips as his hands roamed up and down her back. A small, throaty moan escaped her.

Then his kisses turned from teasing to a hot melding of flesh. As close to making love as was possible fully clothed. Blood rushed everywhere, firing each nerve ending until she could barely keep her knees from buckling.

Caro pressed him harder against her, feeling his masculinity. She wasn't into casual sex at all, but right now, if she weren't expecting workmen, she just might succumb to the fiery heat building in her core. Lifting a knee, she wrapped a leg around him, as if she could pull him any closer.

The world receded and all that mattered this very moment was Max. Here. Kissing her like she was the only woman in his world.

His world.

It wasn't like a douse of cold water, but the thought did bring the world back into focus. Lowering her leg and then unlocking lips, she rested against his chest, breathing hard, wanting more, knowing it was too risky.

"Wow." Max's voice was rough. "What a way to start the morning."

Not trusting her voice, she simply nodded against his oh-so-solid chest.

"I brought bagels and cream cheese and coffee, though it's probably cold by now."

"No problem. After that heat, all I'll have to do is drink it and it'll warm up on the way down."

Max raised her chin and stared at her like she was crazy. Well, she was, and let loose a shaky laugh. "I know, crazy, but that was some kiss."

"There can be more."

It sounded so tempting, so wonderful. So scary.

So impossible.

DAMN, THERE IT WAS AGAIN. THAT SLIGHT PULLING BACK emotionally, the shuttering of her gray eyes.

Why couldn't she see what they had and what it could turn into if she only let it?

"There's a microwave in the closet." He took their paper coffee cups and headed to the utility room behind the staircase.

When he returned, Caro was placing the bagels on opened napkins and had opened the two tubs of cream cheese. Plain and chive. He'd bet she'd go for the chive, and he was the plain old cream cheese guy.

They sat at the long table and sure enough, she smeared the chive spread on her poppy seed bagel.

"Mom's dinner is tonight. I thought I'd pick you up around five-thirty."

She held up a finger, chewed, swallowed, and took a quick sip of coffee. "Yum, good and doughy. That sounds fine. I should be able to get back to the hotel, bathe, and change by then."

Good grief, the vision of her bathing was enough to set him off. He took a sip of his own coffee and nearly choked.

"Okay, so what's the timeline look like for today and tomorrow?"

Max listened to her tick off items without looking at what she called the project bible. She knew exactly what was happening when. He was incredibly impressed with Caro's fierce level of commitment to a project.

"The reason we're going to be ahead of schedule is because of all the treasures I found in Denver. The pieces we bought were like they were made for you."

She handed him the project bible, which she'd updated with images of the receptionist's desk. The desk, the centerpiece, was all sleekness and glass with enough outlets for gadgets and a high-enough ledge that the computer monitor would be shielded from prying eyes.

She'd sketched the glass panels that would hang behind it, including the etched Flatirons.

"I have to update a few more items such as fabric swatches for the furniture, but mostly the bible is complete. And I have a copy on my phone so it's always with me."

"Dedicated."

"Redundant to the point of ridiculous. My key group of people at Forever Young have a copy of the project bible for every job, and they're updated via the cloud all the time. Can't have a crisis and if I'm not there to fix it, nobody else can. That's an operational nightmare."

"And do crises happen often?" he asked, completely fascinated by this side of her. Bohemian and off beat on one side, the other almost OCD in her planning.

"All the time. It's the nature of the biz. Everything from the client wanting last-minute changes, to weather ruining effects, to flowers not being available, to the float breaking down, God forbid."

A visible shudder raced across Caro's shoulders.

"Well, you seem to have everything under control—"

Putting up a hand to stop him, she bent and knocked on the wood floor. "Only wood quickly available," she said, then smiled.

The door opened, letting in a frigid blast. Three men trouped in and introduced themselves. Caro took them to spots where drywall was going up. She was up there a long time but came down with a smile.

"Great news. They can hot-mud the drywall and get it done today. They'd planned to skim the lower offices but now that's moot. Skimming could add another forty-eight hours to the project. It's over a holiday anyway, but I think you're more than fine without it."

"You're the boss."

Putting hands on her hips, she waggled her shoulders. "The staircase will be torn down tonight and the new one installed tomorrow bright and early."

She ran her hands through her hair, tousling it more than usual.

He hated to break the next news to her. "I can't meet for lunch today." Then Max was pleased that she pouted.

"Understand."

"And you're okay with it?"

"No, but—"

Max reached across the table and put a finger to her lips. "Me too. See you tonight."

He couldn't kiss her goodbye as the drywallers were upstairs and down. Giving her a wink, he bundled up and headed out the door. Taking a second to look back and see such longing on her face, he nearly turned back to hold her.

One of the drywallers had a question, and she composed her face and turned to answer him.

Max closed the door gently behind him.

Everything was in her capable hands.

Except him.

13

THE CLOCK READ 6:30 AS CARO SMUDGED THE LAST OF HER eyeshadow. She'd done the impossible. Showered, dried her hair, then slipped on a beaded headband to keep it off her face. Dressed and made up in thirty minutes flat.

She'd already called Max to tell him she'd be late and heard back from him that he'd let his mom know.

Great first impression.

Caro flew down the three flights of stairs to meet Max in the lobby, and in minutes they were driving up Broadway, turning left onto Mapleton Avenue.

"This area is an older part of town."

"Wait." She pointed in wonder at various houses. "These are mansions."

"Some of them. Mapleton Hill was the area where many of Boulder's prominent citizens built their homes. Along with Boulder's earliest schools, the first public library, and the region's first major hospital facility. It's now a historic district."

Max squeezed into the last spot in the driveway. Caro stared with awe at the two-story early 1900s stone home with a huge wrapped porch and a turret. A warm glow in all the windows beckoned them, with a lighted and decorated Christmas tree in the turret room.

She stopped on the stone walkway to admire all the fairy lights in the tall old spruces that framed the house.

Suddenly, Caro felt a tug of longing. Something she'd rarely experienced and yet had felt twice this week. Once at the wedding and now.

To be a part of something. No, make that some*one*. To come home to welcoming lights and warmth. A kiss, a glass of wine as they shared the day.

"Did you grow up in this house?"

"Yep."

"Wow."

"Mom has redone some of it, but mostly it's the same. Remember I told you that her kitchen is much bigger than mine." Max grabbed her hand, and she let herself be led up the stone steps and into the house.

Immediately the sound of voices, the clink of glassware, and the incredible aroma of garlic, tomatoes, herbs, and cheese greeted her.

They walked into a kitchen that, as Max warned her, surpassed both his own and Jen's in size.

The room easily held at least ten people with a few more Caro didn't know in the dining room. Brice and Jen brought Mom and Dad, RJ was in the corner talking to Margo, and a trio seemed to be in deep discussion, looking up as Max called to them.

"Welcome," Geri called, rushing over, spoon in hand, to give her a hug and Max a peck on the cheek. She wore a Christmasy apron that was endearingly cheesy.

"Thank you for having us at your feast," Caro said and totally meant it.

"I love that you're here. Your parents are charming, and your mom has offered to play for us after dinner. RJ and Brice then decided they needed to play, so it could be a long night."

Caro grinned at Geri's faux despair as she left quickly to tend to the pasta.

Brice returned and handed her a glass of cabernet. Jen left Brice and grabbed Caro in a bear hug.

"I can't believe I haven't seen you since the wedding," Caro said, hugging her back.

"Crazy, I know. But we've got tomorrow night off, and by the way, don't forget dinner at our house, then Christmas. Brice is taking your folks to the airport Sunday and I think you were going as well. But I've heard you've changed your plans?"

"Dinner is ready in two, find your places," Geri called to all, interrupting Jen's question.

"Yes, and I'll tell you about it later. I'm staying until the first."

Max linked his arm with hers, and Caro just caught Jen's raised brow and grin.

Hours later after pasta, wine, homemade biscotti, espresso, music, and carol singing, it was time to leave this amazing nest and the people who feathered it.

Sure, she'd been to plenty of parties and work affairs, but this was different. This brought out a loneliness she rarely experienced, intensifying the longing she'd felt when she arrived.

Both emotions made her uncomfortable simply because it seemed to her that both were contrary to her vaunted independence.

Max retrieved her coat and before they left, held her still, then looked up with a question and at her nod, kissed her silly under the mistletoe. A tradition she was instantly fond of.

She felt ... cherished.

"Do we have time to run by Annie's house and see her lights?"

"ABSOLUTELY. I'M NOT IN ANY HURRY FOR THE NIGHT TO END." HE felt Caro's hand clasp his.

Max drove slowly, savoring the night. His time with Caro seemed magnified. They had a bit more than a week together remaining, and somehow he needed to convince her that he was worth returning to. Even staying for.

He understood she had her life and business in California, but she could relocate, right? He couldn't leave Colorado and restart a practice in another state ... *Whoa, dude, listen to yourself. Stop this.*

Caro was the one who could relocate. Period.

Max refused to let any of that ruin the moment. Especially when he turned onto Annie's street and heard Caro's gasp.

"Oh, you weren't kidding. This is totally amazing. It's not the least gaudy—it's a supreme tribute to the magic of Christmas."

Caro's voice vibrated with passion. Damn if he didn't want that same tone when he held her in his arms.

"I'd love to do a float that brings the magic of lights, the star, and her books and characters to life. Hmmmm, maybe I need to contact her agent."

They got out of Max's Porsche and stood in Annie's driveway. Max pointed to the house next door. "That's Cole's house."

Caro's eyes grew wide. "I knew they were neighbors but didn't realize they lived next door. Whose house are they going to live in?"

"Hers. It's bigger, has room for the boys. And if they can, they're going to find a way to see if the city will allow them to combine the lots and agree for Annie to add on to her house. Then Cole can rent out his house."

"Wow, that's complicated, but I bet they know a great attorney."

"I believe they do."

Caro hugged him and raised her face in an invitation he was not going to resist. As it started to snow, he captured her lips with his. Could that be any more perfect? Could Caro leave all this?

Max drove her back to the Boulderado and parked.

"Do you want me to come in?"

"Yes, but you can't. Tomorrow comes early, and honestly, Max, you're way too tempting."

Yes, he fist-pumped mentally. "Then a good night kiss?"

She leaned over the console and pecked his cheek.

Not enough and she knew it, tempting him to respond.

And he did. Turning so their lips met, and kissing her as deeply as he could without holding her against him.

"Dream of me?" he asked, voice husky.

"No question about it."

14

CHRISTMAS EVE DAY. THIS TIME LAST YEAR CARO HAD BEEN fighting one battle after another. The roses she'd ordered for her first big float were late leaving Ecuador. Everything else was on point, but to get those roses trimmed, in their water vials, and on the float, she'd needed more volunteers during the last twenty-four hours in the float barn than she'd scheduled. Her crew had pulled extra hours as well. But everyone was still excited about getting it done by New Year's Day, and their dedication had made it possible for Caro to win the prestigious Princess award.

This Christmas Eve the pressure she felt was all of her own doing. Her "job" was under control. Not so much her emotions. She had just another week in Boulder. She couldn't be here for Max's opening—she had a client meeting on the same day that couldn't be rescheduled. In fact, this client, whose charity was beloved, could be one of her most important clients to date.

Now she was waiting at Max's new office for the crew to arrive and paint the walls of the closets and the wood trim both up and downstairs. Then later this afternoon, the staircase builders needed to do a bit more work and then everyone would head to Christmas Eve and three days off. No more work until Monday.

She bit into her muffin and barely tasted the cinnamon and spice. Max hadn't mentioned seeing her today and the brilliance of the freshly fallen snow dimmed.

But she'd dreamed of him last night as he'd wished. While the setting of the dream was foggy and indistinct, the dream dancing they'd shared felt real. Waking up she was surprised to find she had on her night T-shirt instead of her blue-gray filmy bridesmaid dress flowing around her as they waltzed, pressed body to body.

Caro didn't know how to waltz, but last night she danced.

Her phone rang. She blinked and returned to earth.

"Good morning. How did you sleep?"

Warmth flooded through her hearing Max's husky voice. "Well, I had a dream, but I'm not telling you about it over the phone."

"Not fair. I'm tied up all day. So much for my lightened schedule."

"Patience is a virtue, so they say."

"You're a tease, know that?"

God, she loved their banter. She wondered if it affected him as much as her. "Yeah, I know. So, what are you going to do about it?"

She heard his deep draw of breath.

"I know exactly what I want to do, but ..."

Her heart pounded in her chest. "Now who's the tease?" She heard the husky tone of her voice.

"You're killing me."

"That's not the plan, I want you alive—" Caro broke off. Jeeze, this was a phone call, not a private tête-à-tête.

"Caro?"

"I'm still here. I think we, uh, need to continue this face to face."

"By a fire."

Caro laughed. "Stop."

"Okay, if you will."

"Deal."

There was silence on Max's end. She wondered what he was thinking. Regretting how quickly their conversation turned intimate?

"How late is your dinner at Jen's going to run?"

She blinked. "I have no idea."

Through the phone, she heard the door to his office creak open and a murmur of voices and realized that's why he broke off their conversation.

"Thanks for the information. I'll get back to you later."

Caro smiled at his change of tone, brisk and all business, and decided to turn the tables on him. "Sure thing. And, Max, think about that fire."

Just as she ended the call with a silly smile on her face, the painters entered Max's office building. She crossed the large lobby, introduced herself, and made sure they knew the change in plans. Then she left them to do their job.

She spent the time checking the delivery on all the other items for next week. So far everything was on track. Surprised to see the painters packing up, she realized she'd worked through the afternoon. She glanced at phone and saw zero texts. Darn.

"Merry Christmas," Caro wished them as they were leaving, getting smiles and return Christmas greetings.

Her phone rang and she grinned, hoping it was Max. It wasn't. The staircase carpenters were going to get there, but about an hour late.

Caro decided she needed fresh air, and a trip to the yarn store a few blocks away was the perfect outing. She had plenty of time, but just in case she got engrossed, which was more than possible, she set the timer on her watch. The lovely lady who was there on Caro's first visit wasn't available, but Caro spent a pleasant hour looking at yarn while trying to figure out what Max's color might be. His décor at home was neutrals, no real splash of color anywhere. His kitchen was blond wood and dark quartz countertops. His furniture was fabulous textures of white, caramel, and mahogany. But no throw pillows or afghans.

He wore charcoal and black and it worked on him, but she couldn't use that as his color. It wasn't one. Red wasn't him. She sensed he could be fiery when he needed to, but that wasn't his core personality. Neither were beiges and browns. Green? Nope that was her. All shades of green, blues, and a few grays.

What was the color of success?

As soon as she thought it, she realized that as much as Max felt he needed to showcase his success and that desire colored certain decisions, she figured it was a crutch, something he used as a defense or a shield. He apparently grew up in a wealthy family, so the trappings of success were ingrained. But his mother, while living in a gracious and incredible home, wasn't the least pretentious. In fact, last night she'd reminded Caro to stop by the Carnegie library anytime and, as a volunteer, Geri would be delighted to give her a tour of the archives.

Caro's buzzer went off and she returned to the office empty handed. The carpenters arrived and worked their finishing magic. The staircase was a showpiece. Black iron railings, mahogany steps inlaid with ebony and maple in a craftsman-style motif. She couldn't have designed it better.

Locking the door behind her, she walked the few blocks to Jen's office and met her folks. Jen drove them home, and they reached the house just as Brice arrived.

She so wanted to talk to him and he knew it, but she kept

quiet, knowing this wasn't the time or the place. Maybe they'd have a chance for a brother-sister talk before she left.

"GO, I KNOW YOU WANT TO. I'LL SEE YOU TOMORROW," GERI chided Max ever so gently.

"Caro is with her family. I'm with mine."

"And maybe we'll all be together next year."

Max stared at his mother, mouth slightly agape, until she smiled, and he pulled himself together. Shutting his mouth, he raised his brows. "What on earth gave you that idea?"

"The way you look at her. And the way she smiles at you. You're smitten."

"God, what an old-fashioned word."

"But apt."

Max toyed with his apple crisp. "You know it'll never work. I can't move to California. My practice, my life, is here. Caro's life and work is there. Simple."

"Not simple. Yes, I agree that moving your practice would be hard, but not impossible. Reciprocity is a challenge, but what about taking the California bar?"

"I don't think a part-time relationship would work for either of us."

He didn't like the way his mom nodded, giving up so easily. "Perhaps not. Regardless, go to her and kiss her soundly. Tomorrow is Christmas and you just never know what magic that Flagstaff Star has in store."

Feeling guilty, Max nevertheless rose quickly from the table and bussed his mom on the cheek. "I'll see you for Christmas morning. I love you, Mom."

"Max, I love you too. Wish everyone a merry Christmas from me."

As he drove home, he thought about Dad and how much Mom must miss him. Love was funny. It wormed its way inside your heart and suddenly—

"Damn."

He loved Caro. They didn't know everything about each other yet, so he had to be cautious and let it grow. But he knew if given the chance, this could be a forever love. The kind his mom and dad had. The kind Jen and Brice, Annie and Cole, and Caro's parents had.

Driving past Jen's house, he smiled as all the lights were still on. Not bothering to enter his own house, he closed the garage and headed next door. He knew he could go in the back entrance, but instead he chose to ring the doorbell and wait.

Brice answered. "Hey, perfect timing. We're just having dessert. Everybody, look who's here."

Max smiled and followed Brice into the dining room, zeroing in on Caro's expression. It brightened the minute she realized who the party crasher was.

Brice added a chair to the table next to hers. Astute man.

The warmth of Caro's hand covered his under the table, and he wrapped his fingers around hers and squeezed tight. This was right. He needed to be here with her. Maybe she didn't love him yet, but he was an attorney used to battle and he wasn't giving up on this. It had just begun.

Brandies and conversation spun on until Jen yawned and apologized. Brice was the chauffeur back to the hotel for Caro and her folks. The party broke up as coats, boots, and gloves were donned.

Jen was in the kitchen and Brice and his parents in the garage, so now was the moment. Max was alone with Caro.

Max touched her elbow and she turned. Cupping her face, he traced her cheeks with his thumbs. Then he bent his head and captured her lips with a kiss he hoped would convey wordlessly just what she meant to him. She opened her lips under his and traced his lips ever so lightly with her tongue, branding him forever.

Not bothering to muffle his groan, he pulled her closer, kissing her deeper, telling her that she was his. Her hands ran up and down his back, then she pressed harder against him. He willed their barrier of clothing to disappear, knowing making love with Caro would seal his heart as forever hers.

But that wasn't possible now, so he cherished their kisses and the throaty moan she couldn't hide.

Raising his head, he kept his gaze focused on her, willing her to feel his love. A glimmer of uncertainty in her eyes panicked him, but it vanished so quickly he wondered if he imagined it.

"Caro, my—" he coughed away the word *love.* "Dream of me this Christmas Eve."

"As I have every night since the wedding."

Her husky words made his world right. This ... love was happening very fast yet felt completely real. He'd woo her and together they could figure out how to meld their long-distance lives together.

"Hey, Caro, you ready?" Brice's voice bellowed from the garage.

"Yeah, big brother, be right there."

Caro kissed him lightly. "You dream of me, too, okay?"

"That's a promise."

She grinned and headed for the garage.

Max followed her out and left through the garage, standing there until the taillights of the car disappeared.

Smiling, he walked to his house, didn't bother turning on lights, stripped, and lay in bed, images of Caro playing in his head. Far better than sugar plums any day.

15

CHRISTMAS DAY ARRIVED. CARO HADN'T FELT THIS EXCITED SINCE sixth grade. Sure, Max was going to be at his mom's house along with a passel of neighbors and friends, just as she was going to be with Jen and Brice, Mom and Dad.

But the present Max had given her last night was a sense of being cherished. She was fairly sure he was open to a long-distance relationship, and that's the way she had to have it. So she was getting the best of both worlds. She'd keep her highly prized independence and get the guy. Marriage wasn't in the picture—how could it be? But a relationship with Max, seeing him as often as she could. And her work. Well, life was pretty darn perfect.

Merry Christmas to me.

Brice gave her a souped-up new laptop with wicked speed and magically amazing wireless. This Christmas was guys give the girls presents, a family tradition for alternating years. Brice gave Jen an exquisite yellow diamond pendant, and Dad gave Mom a new shearling coat and fleece-lined boots. Next Christmas it was girls give the guys presents. And then Caro would have something knitted to give Max.

She missed him fiercely, wanting to have him beside her, realizing it was selfish, but still …

Mimosas were passed around as everyone filed into the kitchen to help with brunch.

Caro hung back and tucked her presents of knitted vicuña gloves into her mom's new coat and Jen's vicuña scarf under the tree. It wasn't playing by the rules, but then Caro was already known in the family as the rule breaker.

Her phone rang as she headed for the kitchen. Hoping it was Max, she felt her heart hammering hard against her chest. Then she saw the area code.

A frown wrinkling her brow, she pushed the on button. "This is Caroline Young."

Her heart sank further as she recognized the voice on the other end. "Caroline, Hank Fisher from Children's World Fund. I'm so sorry to call on Christmas Day, but we've decided to double the size of the project for next year and need to move on it now."

This was the opposite of what she'd expected to hear. Shock held her silent.

"Caroline, are you there?"

"Yes, of course. I'm delighted to hear this. I'll be back in the office on Monday the fourth, for the meeting we arranged."

"That won't work. We need to meet tomorrow. We need to secure the funding before the end of this fiscal year, and I know doubling the size will more than double the cost of the float."

"Saturday?"

"Yes, is that a problem?"

"Well, yes. I'm in Colorado and while I can probably catch a flight tomorrow, Sunday is the earliest I can be available."

"I didn't realize you were out of town."

Caro thought quickly. Skiers were flying into Colorado to take advantage of the week between Christmas and New Year.

The airport was sure to be jammed, even getting a flight out could be tricky, but she'd try. "If you don't hear from me, plan on meeting Sunday."

"Thank you. Your office?"

"Yes, around three?"

"And you'll have figures for us."

"Close enough to work into your project budget."

"I'm truly sorry to cut into your vacation, but Children's World Fund wants next year's float to be our biggest and best ever, and we know you're the person to create that."

"Thanks for your confidence. Merry Christmas."

"See you Sunday and Merry Christmas."

The line went dead.

The euphoria Caro felt about the increased float size dimmed as she realized she'd be leaving Max. She wasn't worried about his project since everything was planned, scheduled, and laid out on paper in the project bible with precise detail. The biggest thing was getting someone there to open doors and just oversee it.

She entered the kitchen to face a sea of curious gazes. "Good and bad news. The Children's World Fund has just doubled the size of their float." She smiled at the hoots and hollers of cheer. Then she held up her hand for silence. "The bad news is that I have to leave ... tomorrow."

Silence met her pronouncement. Her gaze zeroed on a face she hadn't seen earlier. Max was in the kitchen? How did he get there?

WHAT THE HELL? A THOUSAND CONFLICTING THOUGHTS RAN through Max's mind at lightning speed. She was leaving him in the lurch? Good for her about the job. But what about them?

What about his plans?

"Congratulations, Caro." He tried hard to keep his voice neutral but could see by her wrinkled brow that she caught his shock before he could mask it.

He'd come over to the house as a surprise, using the back door in the kitchen. He thought maybe he and Caro could head over to his house after the festivities here and have some private time to talk about them.

Their future.

He knew she'd be a tough case to win over, but his feelings for her were clear.

It was love.

The complicated part was that he wanted her in his life.

Did that mean marriage? Was that possible in a long-distance relationship?

Maybe. But right now he wasn't sure even a relationship was possible.

All those thoughts went through his mind before Caro could utter a word.

"Max. You're here."

There it was, strangled. Maybe Caro even sounded guilty.

"Good observation."

Oh, that was mean.

Nevertheless, his attorney training was to remain composed.

This is not law, this is about my heart.

And you blew it. Look at the hurt in her eyes, man.

"We need to talk so I can give you all the details you'll need for Monday," she said flatly.

The kitchen had been deathly quiet, but now Jen started pulling out pans while Brice grabbed ingredients for their brunch from the refrigerator.

"We can go over to my house," Max offered.

"Jen, may we use your office out back?" Caro countered.

"Sure."

Caro led the way and Max followed, still angry, both at himself and the woman in front of him, who practically marched down the stone walkway.

Entering the small office, he saw the plans Caro had drawn still tacked to the wall. It had been only seven days since they'd been in this same room beginning this journey that was now likely going to end here.

Caro moved to the far wall and stood there, arms wrapped around her waist.

"Max, I have to go. I'm sure someone in your office can handle the project bible and make sure the placements are correct. Everything is laid out, so anyone can pick up the bible and use it. That is its purpose."

"I understand that. I don't like it, but I understand it."

"What don't you like, that I'm leaving you? Not in a lurch. You'll be fine. Your office will project just what a brilliant attorney's office should. Success and competence."

"That you're leaving. That I don't know if you'll come back. That there is unfinished business between us."

He saw Caro's mouth form an O.

16

THE MEETING WITH CHILDREN'S WORLD FUND HAD GONE WELL yesterday. Caro had given them enough of a budget they could use to secure the funding and now she was working on expanding the design for the float. She'd been amazed that the parade organization had agreed so quickly to the changes.

Yet, her heart wasn't in it. She wanted to jump a jet and get back to Boulder.

Then do it.

Shaking her head at her inner voice, she fought to concentrate on the design on her computer monitor. It wasn't even eight o'clock in Boulder, yet the need to call her brother Brice and just hear his voice, something she always did when she needed to be grounded, pulsed inside her. She punched in the speed dial number, knowing he'd be awake and maybe at his office.

He picked up on the first ring. "Sis."

"Bro."

"How did the meeting go?"

"Perfect, they even had the go-ahead from the parade

committee, so now I just have to revise and enlarge the float. It'll be something."

"Of that I have no doubt."

Caro didn't know how to broach the subject of Max with her brother, so she let the silence play out.

"How do you feel about Max?"

"That's pretty direct," she said, and heard Brice's chuckle. "He's the first man I've met that I really connected with. Smart, funny, a bit too concerned about the trappings of what he thinks looks like success. But he's ... Oh, Brice, I think I'm really falling in love with him."

"And why is that an issue?"

"He's there, I'm here. And anyway, I think he's more upset than he let on about me not being there to finish the job I started for him."

"Caro, Jen and I are often out of town. That's the nature of our separate jobs. Vader has me running all over the world, and Jen, well, she's always on the go with the amount of computer hacking that's happening today. Her forensics biz is going through the roof. We make it work because we know that our jobs are part of who we are. If I tried to make her quit or change or vice versa, we'd end up a broken couple."

"I know. But you're a rare couple."

"Not so rare these days. We make the time we do spend together important. Do I miss her when we're apart? You bet. Do we talk on the phone and text when we can? Yes, even using those silly emoticons. The point is that relationships in today's world are not the same as they were even ten years ago. It takes work to make it happen, but then all relationships do.

"If you think you love him, you need to find out. Then see if you can find the common ground necessary to make it work. Love is a great common denominator. And, Caro, your need for independence doesn't have to disappear. It's part of you. It just means independence isn't tied to loneliness."

Caro let the words play out, and then realized Brice was still on the phone. "Love you. Thanks. Bye." Again, she heard his chuckle and the line went dead.

MAX WATCHED THE INSTALLATION OF THE SLEEK NEW receptionist's desk and marveled again at just how perfectly Caro had nailed the juxtaposition of old with modern. The glass panels that would hang behind it would come tomorrow.

"What do you think, is this the right place?"

Margo held her photo of the Flatirons up to the wall opposite where glass panels etched with the same image would hang.

"Let me check the book."

He looked at the precise measurements Caro had neatly printed on that page and grabbed the tape measure to make sure they had it right. "Up about here." He pointed, and Margo marked the spot.

The installation of the desk finished up. "We'll have the coffee station in tomorrow," one of the guys said, and the team left.

"Too bad the elevator won't be in for a couple of months, but it's a great idea. Variance or not. You made the right decision to do it, even with the extra cost."

"Yeah."

"Max?"

He looked at Margo and recognized the concern on her face. He wasn't usually so taciturn. "It's okay."

"I don't think it is, but it's your life. Just don't let your stubbornness get in the way. I'm heading home. I'll be here tomorrow for a couple hours in the morning, and actually Jen is going to be here in the afternoon."

Margo bundled up and left. It had been snowing since dawn, and normally the beauty of it gave him a lot of pleasure. Now all he could remember was how much Caro loved it.

And that he couldn't share it with her. Even if it was only by a photo attached to a text or a phone call.

"The desk looks great. I hope you like it."

Max stood still, wondering for a nanosecond if he'd imagined Caro's voice.

Then he turned to find her standing in the doorway as if unsure whether she'd be welcomed back.

And he realized in that flash that she'd come back. Covering the short distance in a few long strides, he wrapped her in a hug and pulled her into the foyer. Closing the door with a shove of his foot, he twirled her around.

"Nothing looks better than you being right here, right now."

"Max—"

"Caro—"

She pulled a dark steel-blue muffler from her pocket and wrapped it around his neck. "I found your color. Finished it on the plane."

Smiling, he fingered the soft wool. But instead of talking, he let his heart speak and captured her lips in a kiss he hoped would show how much he loved her.

He had no idea how long they stood, arms entwined. But it could never be long enough for him.

"Wow, I hope you don't meet all your designers that way," Caro said, her voice as breathless as he felt.

"Nope."

"Good, because I'd hate to be building up all these airline miles I think I'm going to accumulate and have them go to waste."

"We can take vacations with them."

"Hawaii?"

"Do you want to try?" Max asked, his voice rough.

"I never just try, I do. But I admit I'm a bit nervous."

"About us?"

"About blending our lives together."

Max tapped a finger to her lips. "I understand, I do. This is new to both of us, but—"

He felt Caro's finger on his lips, mimicking his earlier touch on hers.

"Maximillian Henderson III, I love you. My dream on Christmas Eve is coming true."

"Caroline Young, you breathe joy and color into my life. I love you."

"That too was part of my dream."

~ The End ~

LETTER TO MY READERS

I started this journey with a single book, *Be Mine This Christmas Night*, because Christmas holds a special place in my heart. Then the other characters in the book begged me to tell their stories, and this series, Star Light ~ Star Bright, was born.

Christmas has remained a special season for me, from the wonder of believing in Santa Claus as a child to the wonder of believing in the kindness and grace of the season as an adult. And since living in Boulder, Colorado, the wonder of the star on Flagstaff mountain.

Love and forgiveness seem more significant at this time of year as well.

If you enjoyed this story, please leave a review on the store's review site where you purchased it. And if you can at BookBub and Goodreads as well. We writers live or die by reviews. I know it sounds dramatic but it is so true. This is the way readers find us and buy the book.

Also, on my website www.lesliesartor.com, you can find entire *Star Light ~ Star Bright* series on the "Book Shelf" page.

And I have a newsletter that enjoy writing and sending monthly. Keeping you up to date on my writing, my crazy busy life and often my photography. And don't forget, I love hearing from you via email!

ACKNOWLEDGMENTS

I've said repeatedly I have trusted people who help me make my books the best they can be.

Audra Harders, who always believes that I can pull a story together and make it shine. We've been writing buddies for two-plus decades.

Amanda Cabot, who is always finding ways to make my stories stronger.

And two of the **Three Book Babes** (I'm number three), Nancy Haddock and Neringa Bryant, who bucked me up, told me I could do this and then gave me the time and space at our annual retreat to do just that.

Ellis Vidler, my editor, who makes my stories shine. Truly my rock when I lose my way in a story. Thank you.

I can't leave out my darling **Mom,** who even with macular degeneration, reads my books to proof them for left out words, etc. before I go to publication.

And of course, my husband **Gary**, who never gives me any grief about my hours in front of the computer, talking out loud and needing a new monitor, printer or whatever I need to do what I love. Babe, you're the best.

ALSO BY L. A. SARTOR

STAR LIGHT ~ STAR BRIGHT

A Romantic Christmas Series Set In Snowy Boulder, Colorado

Be Mine This Christmas Night

Forever Yours This New Year's Night

Believe In Me This Christmas Morn

Dream Of Me This Christmas Eve

THE CARSWELL ADVENTURE SERIES

Heart Pounding Adventure & Romance Set In Exotic Locales

Stone Of Heaven

Viking Gold

THE KAHUNA GROUP

Romantic Suspense With Powerful, Professional Investigators-Offices in Hawaii ~ Denver ~ Los Angeles

Dare To Believe

Brushed By Betrayal

THE PLANTATION SERIES

Pure Romance Set in Costa Rica On A Rare Cacao Plantation

Prince Of Granola

THE JENNA HART JEWELRY MYSTERIES

A Cozy Mystery Series Set in the Colorado Ski Town Of Angelcroft

Tick Tock Dead (coming soon)

Capture the code with a mobile device's QR reader to see all of
L.A. Sartor's Books

ABOUT L.A. SARTOR

I started writing as a child, really. A few things happened on the way to becoming a published author ... specifically, a junior high school teacher who told me I couldn't write because I didn't want to study ... urk ... grammar.

That English teacher stopped my writing for years. But the muse couldn't be denied, and eventually I wrote, a lot, some of it award winning. However, I wasn't really making a career from any of this.

My husband told me repeatedly that independent publishing was becoming a valid way to publish a novel. I didn't believe him even after he showed me several *Wall Street Journal* articles. I thought indie meant vanity press.

I couldn't have been more wrong.

I started pursuing this direction seriously, hit the keyboard, learned a litany of new things and published my first novel. My second book became a bestseller, and I'm absolutely on the right course in my life.

I live in Colorado with my husband Gary whom I met on a blind date—I can't imagine life without my best friend. We play in the mountains and travel as much as possible.

Find me at www.lasartor.com

BE MINE THIS CHRISTMAS NIGHT

STAR LIGHT ~ STAR BRIGHT SERIES
BOOK ONE

GLANCING AT THE CROWD BUNDLED UP AGAINST THE NEAR ZERO-degree December evening as they gathered in the street, on the sidewalk, the neighbor's yards—wherever there was room—Annabelle Hamilton grinned. She loved the anticipation building toward the moment the thousands of lights adorning her home would be turned on.

Showtime.

With her hand on the switch, she scanned the crowd one more time and caught sight of a small, solitary figure standing outside the house of her new next-door neighbor.

She knew two young boys lived there, so perhaps he was one of the kids. But why was the house dark when she was sure everyone was home and it was far too early for the boys to be in bed? And why didn't he just come over, instead of hiding in the shadows?

"Annie? Everyone is waiting."

The nudge on her shoulder from one of the twin brothers who helped her hang the thousands of lights pulled her attention back to the big moment.

"Sorry. See that kid over there?" Annie pointed, but the child had left.

Shaking away her puzzlement, she held her breath and flipped the electrical switch.

The ooohs and ahhhs reflected her own thrill at seeing the brilliant magic of light sparkling everywhere. Especially the huge stars that arrived special delivery a few hours ago. The twins had worked feverishly to get them hung, and the stars were spectacular, glimmering high in the tall linden, looking as if they'd just fallen from the sky to hover in her tree.

The applause started and swelled, and someone in the crowd began singing the Christmas carol "Joy to the World." Annie joined in, belting it out for all she was worth.

Her daddy established this tradition of decorating with lights on one particularly rough Christmas as a way to cheer her up, and it worked. Every Christmas since that long-ago year, hope symbolized by light had been a part of her celebration. Even when she lived in the old homestead in the backwoods of Maine and she was the only person around to enjoy her effort. Just her and the critters.

She turned back to look at her home of the last four years, nestled close to Chautauqua Park in Boulder, Colorado. The tingle of pride, followed by the warm contentment she always felt when pulling into the driveway, was magnified tonight.

The steep eaves were defined by miniature white lights, while the bushes and trees out front and in her backyard were strung with hundreds more of the little bulbs.

Just before she ducked under the peaked roof of her carport to begin ladling the hot cider bubbling in the crock pot, Annie glanced once more at the dark house next door.

Her neighbor had moved in more than a month ago, and by the buff look of him, she figured he was some sort of pro athlete or maybe a sports manager.

From her second-floor bedroom window, she'd unabashedly watched him flex and lift as the pile of boxes from the U-Haul dwindled. Sweat glistened on his forehead even in the winter chill. The next time he came out of the house, a sweat band held back his ebony hair, and he'd pulled off his sweatshirt, revealing a gray T-shirt with cutoff sleeves, the front emblazoned with a faded "Black's Gym, Chantilly, Virginia" emblem.

Another man was traipsing in and out of the house, spending most of his time helping the kids with their smaller boxes or keeping them out of the way of the hunk. Annie wondered who the second man was.

And the boys, they were adorable. She'd guess they were around seven and nine, and she couldn't wait to meet them properly.

Probably not tonight, she regretted, glancing again at the dark windows. Maybe they'd gone to bed early to avoid the chaos. But chaos was part of the lighting celebration, and she'd made a point of putting a flier in her new neighbor's mailbox announcing her "Annual Christmas Lighting" dates and the warning that the lights were on from dusk to dawn.

So maybe he hated Christmas lights, but Annie would bet her bottom dollar those boys would have been as entranced by the lights as she'd been when she was a wee girl and her daddy turned them on each season.

A collective cheer went up from the crowd as the surly gray clouds that had been gathering and building all day finally let loose their treasure of white fluffy flakes.

She moved from underneath the shelter of the carport and looked upward, letting the cold flakes land on her face. "Thanks, Daddy," she whispered.

"Who are you talking to?"

Annie glanced down to see which of the many

neighborhood kids was addressing her, surprised to find it was the younger of the two boys from next door.

She looked at the house, the lights still dark. Maybe he'd been the one standing alone in the shadows. Which meant his father most likely didn't know he was outside in the frigid cold.

Guiding him under the carport to the cider table and a bit of warmth, Annie chose her answer carefully. "I was just saying thanks to my daddy for sending the snow."

"Is he in heaven?"

"I like to think of him sitting on a star high in the sky, so yes, if that's heaven, that's where he is."

"My mommy's in heaven too, but I don't think she's on a star. I don't know where she is."

Annie hadn't realized the man next door was a widower. "Has your mommy been gone long?"

"Forever."

"Two years, Josh. Don't exaggerate."

Annie spun to her left to see her new neighbor in his buttoned-up black wool overcoat, complete with a dark gray muffler wrapped around his neck, looming over the table, irritation written all over his face.

"Excuse me, but would you mind moving a bit farther to your left?" she asked.

He looked baffled at her request, and she didn't care that she was less than polite—his brusque answer to his son instantly raised her hackles.

COLE EVANS TOOK IN THE MIGHTY MOUSE IN FRONT OF HIM, HIS son's crestfallen face, the line forming behind him and stepped left.

"Thank you," mighty mouse said, not bothering to look at him.

His petite neighbor handed a steaming cup of cider to an elderly woman he'd seen around the neighborhood once or twice since moving in. Then a couple of kids got cups carefully filled only halfway so that the hot liquid wouldn't spill and burn them if they jiggled the cup.

Something he'd never have thought about, and Lauren would have. His brother-in-law, Mitch, was right—Cole did need him to help while he learned how to be a solo parent.

"Would you like some?"

His neighbor was offering Josh cider, but not him. Cole grinned, he couldn't help it. Somehow, he'd made her mad, and they'd not even formally met. Yet.

Josh looked at him for permission to accept the cider, and he nodded.

After his son finished drinking from his carefully cradled cup, Cole figured it was time to introduce himself and make a graceful exit out of the crush of people gawking at the light display. It reminded him of a play opening on Broadway. Not at all what he'd expected when he learned an author lived next door.

He thought of authors as solitary people, living in their own world, creating characters, playing with their lives, and maybe giving them a happy ending.

He extended his hand. "I'm Dr. Cole Evans and this is my younger son, Josh."

The petite woman in front of him stared like he'd grown two heads. What had he said?

"Author Annabelle Hamilton."

Ah, the whole formal name thing, complete with his PhD. He had to remember where he was living now, the part of the country where that kind of formality was reserved for colleagues, and usually only for the first introduction.

He lowered his hand. "Oh, sorry, it's an East Coast thing."

"Chantilly, Virginia?"

"How did you know that?"

"Your gym T-shirt."

As soon as the words left her lips, her eyes widened and her gaze flew to his.

Why? When had he last worn his gym shirt outside?

Moving in.

His smile broadened. She immediately looked away him, obviously embarrassed by her revelation. Cole followed her gaze to see Josh staring at her, bug-eyed.

"Are you the star books lady?"

No, please no. Cole closed his eyes. A hard lump tightened his throat at his son's wistful question.

Josh adored those books. Lauren had read one or another of the dozens of short books to him every night. For a while after Lauren died, Cole tried to keep up the ritual, but work kept him coming home later and later, and often Josh was asleep.

His son wouldn't let their housekeeper read to him, and Mitch didn't pick up the practice. Every once in a while, Cole would find a book tucked in the sheets when he woke his son. A reminder of how much they'd all lost when Lauren died.

Cole refocused on the present.

Annabelle bent so she could be face to face with his son. "Yes, I'm the star books lady. Do you read my books?"

"Some of them. Some are too hard."

"Well, I can help you with the words, so come on over any time."

"Really?"

"Yup. And, Josh, call me Annie, okay? Although I'm thinking being called 'star books lady' is pretty darn cool."

The woman hadn't bothered to glance Cole's way again after she'd inadvertently revealed her peeping. And now she was issuing invitations to his son without his consent? *And when did that start to be an issue with you?*

Just now.

Damn.

The mighty mouse standing in from of him was no doubt a very pretty lady, especially with a thousand twinkling lights highlighting those reddish tints in her short dark hair. The bulky parka did nothing to diminish her petite figure, and her eyes reminded him of the rich whiskey he and Mitch often drank once the boys were asleep.

Stop cataloging her features. You're not going there, remember?

But he didn't want her to start being buddies with his son.

Why?

Because she's a woman.

Well, that's just stupid.

Cole turned to his son, using him as an excuse to get the heck away. "Time to go."

"Aw, Dad, just a little bit longer," Josh pleaded.

"Son, you left the house without permission, so no. And according to the flier Ms. Hamilton left us, you'll be able to see the lights until New Year's," he said, knowing his tone was a bit too sharp and his son would cajole him daily about seeing either Annie or the lights.

Damn.

"Do you have a problem with that?" Annabelle asked.

Cole raised a brow at the challenge in her voice.

"No, I'm a believer in blackout curtains."

～

Annie's jaw dropped, and it was only after Dr. Cole Evans and Josh had reached the end of her driveway that she thought of a good comeback. "I've heard vampires sleep like that," she muttered.

The arrogance of the man.

Just then Jenny Malone, her best friend and the reason she moved to Boulder, burst onto the scene.

"Who's a vampire? I'm sorry I'm late—the traffic backed up on 36 the minute the flakes began falling. Who was the good-looking man that just stormed out of here?"

Annie smiled at Jen's non-stop run of words. Irrepressible and a brilliant digital forensic expert, Jen was constantly on the go, and unless it was business, she was always ten to fifteen minutes late.

"The vampire."

At Jenny's quizzical look, Annie told the truth. "That was my new neighbor."

"Seriously? Wow. What did you do to put a scowl on that gorgeous face?"

"Why would you think I'd done something?"

Annie grinned at her friend's raised brow. "Celebrate the season with lights? Be an author his son loves? Be a woman? I have no idea."

Jenny pursed her lips and started ladling out the cider, taking the job from Annie.

As Annie left the cover of the carport to mingle and enjoy the lights, she called back, "And he's a widower," smiling wider when Jen's eyes grew large and her friend waggled her brows.

Despite Jenny's obvious insinuation that her neighbor was yummy and maybe available, Annie had no intention of finding out. Josh was adorable, and she'd love having him visit, but Cole? Not so much.

Anyway, it was obvious that *Dr. Cole Evans* was enamored of his medical degree and its status. She wasn't. Her daddy had always been known as Doc Hamilton and was introduced that way by people who knew him, but she'd never heard him introduce himself any other way than Adam Hamilton.

Annie stopped thinking about her neighbor and recaptured the feeling of wonder as she walked among the crowds, admiring her celebration of the season.

Finally the cars blocking the street began to thin, and Jenny joined her as she walked across the road to enjoy her lights from a distance. The stark difference between her lighted wonderland and Cole Evans's house was unsettling.

Maybe they didn't celebrate Christmas, but then, her lights weren't strictly about Christmas—more about the peace and hope of the holiday.

The snow fell harder, and Annie let it lay on her jacket and hair where it landed, relishing the essence of winter. She'd spent a year in Florida and missed Colorado's diverse changing of the seasons.

She swiftly considered the merits of each season. After it snowed, winter's short days were often sun-kissed because of Boulder's high altitude.

Spring and its indecision of whether it was winter or summer as the crocus emerged—the first harbingers of the new season—only to have snow blanketing them the next day.

Summer with temps high enough for tubing in Boulder Creek, intensely blue skies, shorts, riding a bike and homemade lime popsicles.

And with fall came the expectancy of the winter, yet the remnants of summer still lifted the temperatures so the days often made wearing shorts still in order.

Yes, she loved all the seasons, but as she admired her lights, Annie admitted winter and Christmas had the edge.

A light flickered on in a room at the Evans' household,

drawing her attention. A small figure stood at the window, blackout curtains pulled aside, looking toward her house.

Josh probably couldn't see her standing across the street, but she saw him for a second as the lights of her house played on his face, and the yearning written there tore at her heart.

The lights went off, and the curtain dropped as Josh abruptly turned around, apparently caught in the act.

"Too bad," she murmured.

"What?" Jenny asked.

"Josh, the vampire's youngest son. He seems to really want to —" Annie stamped her cold feet, now getting numb as she searched to find the right words.

"He wants to be a part of this, of Christmas, and his father seems to be trying to make sure he doesn't."

She braved Jenny's stare, then turned to match it. "To quote you, 'What?'"

"Don't start with them. If the father is a widower, and the boy—or at least the little one—misses the mother horribly, then getting involved with the son will only bring you heartache. Face it, kiddo, you're not their mother. And it won't bring the father to your side either."

"I don't want the father, but I do want Josh to enjoy the season."

"I'm warning you, it's trouble."

Annie slipped her hand through her friend's arm and headed back to her house. "Time for a glass of wine. I want to show you my new story."

"You're changing the subject, but I'm up for wine. Just remember, you're going to make trouble if you get involved."

www.ingramcontent.com/pod-product-compliance
Lightning Source LLC
Chambersburg PA
CBHW030633130626
46552CB00002B/826